W9-DIG-847

The Extinction of the
Dinosaurs

The Extinction of the
Dinosaurs

New and future titles in the series include:

The Mystery Library

The Extinction of the
Dinosaurs

Don Nardo

Lucent Books, Inc.
P.O. Box 289011, San Diego, California

On cover: Tyrannosaurus rex fleeing an asteroid impact 65 million years ago on the Yucatan Peninsula in Central America.

Library of Congress Cataloging-in-Publication Data

Nardo, Don, 1947–
    The extinction of the dinosaurs / by Don Nardo.
        p. cm. — (The mystery library)
    ISBN 1-56006-890-6 (alk. paper)
    1. Dinosaurs—Juvenile literature. 2. Extinction
(Biology)—Juvenile literature. [1. Dinosaurs. 2. Extinction
(Biology)] I.Title. II. Series: Mystery library (Lucent Books)
    QE861.6.E95N37 2002
    567.9—dc21
                                             2001001769

Copyright 2002 by Lucent Books, Inc.
P.O. Box 289011, San Diego, California 92198-9011

Printed in the U.S.A.

Contents

Foreword

In Shakespeare's immortal play, *Hamlet*, the young Danish aristocrat Horatio has clearly been astonished and disconcerted by his encounter with a ghost-like apparition on the castle battlements. "There are more things in heaven and earth," his friend Hamlet assures him, "than are dreamt of in your philosophy."

Many people today would readily agree with Hamlet that the world and the vast universe surrounding it are teeming with wonders and oddities that remain largely outside the realm of present human knowledge or understanding. How did the universe begin? What caused the dinosaurs to become extinct? Was the lost continent of Atlantis a real place or merely legendary? Does a monstrous creature lurk beneath the surface of Scotland's Loch Ness? These are only a few of the intriguing questions that remain unanswered, despite the many great strides made by science in recent centuries.

Lucent Books' Mystery Library series is dedicated to exploring these and other perplexing, sometimes bizarre, and often disturbing or frightening wonders. Each volume in the series presents the best-known tales, incidents, and evidence surrounding the topic in question. Also included are the opinions and theories of scientists and other experts who have attempted to unravel and solve the ongoing mystery. And supplementing this information is a fulsome list of sources for further reading, providing the reader with the means to pursue the topic further.

The Mystery Library will satisfy every young reader's fascination for the unexplained. As one of history's greatest scientists, physicist Albert Einstein, put it:

> The most beautiful thing we can experience is the mysterious. It is the source of all true art and science. He to whom this emotion is a stranger, who can no longer wonder and stand rapt in awe, is as good as dead: his eyes are closed.

Solving the "Crime" of the Dinosaurs' Death

Monsters once roamed the earth, awesome creatures so numerous, diverse, and successful that they ruled the planet for some 160 million years, more than two hundred times longer than human beings have existed. Some of these creatures were huge herbivores (plant eaters) weighing thirty or more tons, giants whose footsteps shook the ground; others were carnivores (meat eaters) with razor-sharp teeth and muscular legs that allowed them to charge at and chase down prey; still others grew feathers and took to the air, becoming the first birds. When scientists first began to discover the remains of these bizarre but impressive beasts, they concluded that they were reptiles and so named them "dinosaurs," meaning "terrible lizards."

The Mystery of the Dinosaurs' Doomsday

The scientists also eventually came to the conclusion that the dinosaurs had all died out at roughly the same time—approximately 65 million years ago. This marked the end of what experts call the Mesozoic era (the era of "middle life"). What could have caused the sudden demise of so many apparently successful and flourishing species all over the world, the scientists wondered? As if this were not mysterious enough, paleontologists (scientists who study ancient life) found that the dinosaurs had not faced their doomsday alone. At least 70 percent of all animal and plant species on earth had perished at the same time.

Many paleontologists and other scientists naturally tried to solve this mystery, which also came to fascinate many non-scientists as well. In the past 150 years or so, thousands of articles and books (fiction as well as nonfiction) have advanced all manner of causes for the great late Mesozoic extinction. In 1964, well before the list of these causes was complete, Princeton University scientist Glenn Jepsen compiled the following summary of the more prevalent and colorful theories:

These two Dryptosauri, *also called* Laelops *meaning "the leaper," had the ability to jump high above the ground. In theory, small dinosaurs with this ability may eventually have taken to the air and become birds.*

Authors of varying competence have suggested that dinosaurs disappeared because the climate deteriorated (became suddenly or slowly too hot or cold or dry or wet), or their diet did (with too much food or not enough of such substances as fern oil; from poisons in water or plants or ingested minerals; by bankruptcy of calcium or other necessary elements). Other writers have put the blame on disease, parasites, wars, anatomical or metabolic disorders (slipped vertebral discs, malfunction or imbalance of hormone and endocrine systems, dwindling brain and consequent stupidity, heat, sterilization, effects of being warm-blooded in the Mesozoic world), racial old age . . . changes in the pressure or composition of the atmosphere, poison gases, volcanic dust, excessive oxygen from plants, meteorites, comets, gene pool drainage by little mammalian egg-eaters, overkill capacity by predators, fluctuation of gravitational constants [i.e., changes in the pull of gravity], development of psychotic suicidal factors . . . cosmic radiation, shift of earth's poles, floods, continental drifts, extraction of the moon from the Pacific Basin, drainage of swamp and lake environments, sunspots, God's will, mountain building, raids by little green hunters in flying saucers, [and even] lack of . . . standing room in Noah's Ark. [1]

Modern Sleuths Encounter Difficulty

The extraordinary size and diversity of this list shows that the mystery of the dinosaurs' demise intrigued, frustrated, and ultimately stumped the scientific community for a long time. It is natural to ask why the riddle was so difficult to solve. First and foremost, bones and other kinds of ancient evidence for dinosaurs are extremely scarce and difficult to interpret, so formulating clear-cut, believable, and definitive answers to riddles about these beasts is not easy. According to James L. Powell of the Los Angeles County Museum of Natural History,

A paleontologist chips away at rocks encasing an ancient dinosaur skeleton. Unfortunately, most dinosaur remains disappeared long ago, and modern scientists have found relatively few of these beasts' bones for study.

In the historical sciences—geology, archaeology, paleontology—definitive answers are particularly hard to come by. Scientists in these fields do not have the advantage of being able to design and then conduct experiments, as is done in chemistry, physics, and many areas of biology. Rather, they have to operate more as detectives. The "experiments" were conducted long ago by nature; scientists working today literally must pick up the pieces and try to interpret them. A "crime"—in this case dinosaur extinction—is discovered, sometimes by accident. In the mystery novel, the clues accumulate and, before we realize it, the clever detective has identified the culprit. But the mysteries of the earth, like real crimes, are not always so easily solved. . . . We can learn about prehistoric animals only from their fossilized remains, and yet many had no hard parts and therefore left no trace. . . . Other organisms were bony; but all too often, before they could be fossilized, their bones dissolved or weathered away. The fossils that did form had a way of winding up in rocks other than those in which, millions of years later, we happen to be searching. . . . To take a different kind of example, in the winter after the great Yellowstone [National Park] fires of 1988, thousands of elk perished from extreme cold coupled with lack of food. Late the following spring, their carcasses were strewn everywhere. Yet only a few years later, bones from the great elk kill are scarce. The odds that a single one will be preserved so that it can be found 65 million years from now approach zero.[2]

Another reason the great dinosaur extinction puzzle was so hard to piece together was that scientists had long worked under certain assumptions that turned out to be mistaken. Most significantly, they assumed that the natural processes observable on earth have always operated the way they do today. The rise and fall of seas, the drifting of the continents, erosion of hillsides, and so on all happen very slowly, and thousands and often millions of years must pass before they add up to major changes. Whatever killed the dinosaurs, the general reasoning went, must have been fairly gradual, too. Therefore, scientists tended to dismiss out-of-hand sudden, rare, catastrophic events—such as asteroids striking the earth—as possible dinosaur killers.

This line of reasoning was unfortunate, for today a majority of scientists are convinced that the catastrophic effects of the impact of an asteroid or comet destroyed the dinosaurs.

Although a few dissenters remain, the consensus is that the object hurtled out of the sky at supersonic speeds and crashed to the earth, blasting out a monstrous hole some one hundred miles in diameter and forty miles deep. The enormous effects and by-products of the blast then wiped out much of the life on earth, including the dinosaurs, in the following weeks and months.

Piecing together the dramatic and startling scenario was no simple task. After more than a century of searching and conjecture, a handful of researchers stumbled on the initial evidence for this fateful impact. Through arduous, painstaking

A Tyrannosaurus rex, *mightiest of the dinosaurian meat eaters, unaware of impending doom in this dramatic reconstruction of the last second before the great impact that most scientists believe wiped out the dinosaurs.*

efforts, they and a growing number of their colleagues eventually found the impact to be, in the words of scientist Gregory S. Paul, "far and away the leading candidate"[3] for the dinosaurs' extinction.

The story of how science tentatively solved this greatest of all dinosaur riddles reads like a classic murder mystery novel. First came the dastardly crime; then the detectives hunted for evidence and considered a number of suspects; finally, an unexpected trail of provocative clues led them to accuse an unlikely suspect; and he turned out to be guilty.

Chapter 1

The First Great Dinosaur Mystery

The first person credited with finding part of what is now recognized as a dinosaur was an English country doctor and amateur geologist named Gideon Mantell. Actually, the credit should probably go to his wife, Mary. According to the popular but still unsubstantiated story of the discovery, in 1822 Mary spied a large tooth poking out of a rock pile near a roadside and brought it to her husband. He supposedly exclaimed, "You have found the remains of an animal new to science."[4]

Beginning with this and the other early discoveries of their remains, dinosaurs were wrapped in an air of mystery. This is not surprising considering that before these finds the scientific community had never even dreamed that such creatures had ever existed. It is important to emphasize that the initial mystery about the dinosaurs was not how they had become extinct but, rather, *if* they had become extinct. The fact is that at first no one knew exactly what these beasts were or when they had lived. More important, the first major dinosaur discoveries were made at a time when the very idea of biological species becoming extinct was extremely controversial.

To uncover and identify the mystery of what killed the dinosaurs, therefore, scientists first had to solve the mystery of whether the process of extinction was real or simply a flight of the imagination. If extinction was a false premise, dinosaur bones were simply the remains of previously unknown creatures, some of which might still be living. On the other hand, if extinction was a real natural process, these bones might represent the discovery of a whole new class of animals that had occupied the earth long before humans arose, which would open up exciting new vistas for scientific study.

Extinction Not Part of God's Plan?

In fact, most scientists' rejection of the idea of extinction before the early nineteenth century was what kept dinosaurs from being properly identified long before. People had been unearthing unusual fossil bones in Europe and Asia at least since the 1500s. One of the more famous such finds was a large thighbone dug up in Oxfordshire, England, in 1677. Experts now know that this bone belonged to a dinosaur. But at the time no one suspected its true nature. Indeed, in those days the fact that various fossils seemed to come from previously unknown animals did not necessarily indicate that the beasts had lived long ago and then become extinct. It was more likely, scientists said, that the descendants of these creatures had migrated away from Europe and that some of them still existed in unexplored regions of the earth. Another commonly advanced explanation was that the odd fossils were the remains of freaks of nature, unusually large or deformed versions of known animals.

This flat rejection of extinction came from the scientists' unquestioned acceptance of religious explanations for the creation of the world and animal species. Before the nineteenth century, the vast majority of Europeans strictly adhered to the teachings of the Bible. They saw this book as the direct word of God and, thus, infallible. The Bible clearly describes the stages in which God created the heavens, earth, plants, animals, and humans.

One of the most common and persuasive arguments for this religious explanation of creation was known as the "argument from design." It contended that nature and everything within it made up a system so incredibly complex and perfectly interactive that it must have been designed by a being of superior intelligence, and that being could be none other than God. The argument from design was most eloquently stated by eighteenth-century theologian William Paley in his 1802 treatise, *Natural Theology, or Evidences for the Existence and Attributes of the Deity Collected from the Appearances of Nature.* Paley used the now-famous analogy of a watch someone finds on the ground. Comparing the workings of the watch to the workings of nature, he stated that one had to conclude

The fossilized spine of a dinosaur protrudes from a layer of limestone unearthed at Dinosaur National Monument, in Colorado.

> that the watch must have had a maker; that there must
> have existed, at some time and at some place or other,

an artificer [maker] or artificers, who formed it for the purpose which we find it actually to answer; who comprehended its construction, and designed its use. . . . Every indication of contrivance, every manifestation of design, which existed in the watch, exists in the works of nature; with the difference, on the side of nature, of being greater or more, and that in a degree which exceeds all computation.[5]

Reinforcing this argument were passages from the Bible itself. According to the Book of Ecclesiastes (3:14), for example, "Whatsoever God doeth, it shall be forever: Nothing can be put to it, nor any thing taken from it." The meaning of this passage seemed all too clear to believers. God's handiwork, including animals, was meant to last forever, and no new species could be created without his intervention. Species also could not die out unless God willed it, so the naturally occurring extinction of a species must be impossible. An alternate explanation for the creation of living things was seen as blasphemous (against God) and therefore unthinkable.

Assumptions About the Age of the Earth

Another factor that kept scientists from recognizing the true nature of dinosaur fossils was their ignorance about the ages of both the fossils and the earth itself. The concept of strange animal species roaming the earth millions of years ago did not initially occur to people because of the widespread belief that the earth was very young. In fact, given the information supplied in the Bible, it appeared to be only a few thousand years old.

In 1650, a Protestant theologian named James Ussher examined the generations of the patriarchs, priests, judges, and kings listed in the Old Testament. From his calculations, he concluded that the creation had occurred in 4004 B.C., and Noah's flood in 2349 B.C. A few years later, the noted English scholar John Lightfoot confirmed the bishop's general calculations and issued a slightly refined version. According to

In Gustave Dore's famous engraving, Noah sends forth a dove from the Ark. Before scientists accepted the premise of biological extinction, they fell back on such biblical stories to explain many natural phenomena.

Lightfoot, the creation had taken place at exactly 9:00 A.M. on Sunday, October 23, 4004 B.C.

Under the time constraints imposed by the religious view of the creation, there had not been time for the species created so recently to become extinct. Therefore, very few people even considered such concepts. And those who did felt obligated to make their observations of nature conform to the accepted orthodox view that the world was only about six thousand years old. However, this did not stop a few from suspecting that the earth was much older. All around them—in fossils, in sea sediments, in rock layers beneath the ground—scholars increasingly saw evidence that the earth was in fact very ancient. But religion's hold on society was so strong that some scientists ignored this evidence outright.

Other scholars tried to reconcile the geologic evidence with biblical statements and calculations. They suggested that the world was indeed much older than Bishop Ussher had decreed but that God had not revealed this fact in the Bible. According to this view, God had originally created certain species and then destroyed them in Noah's flood. By keeping Noah from preserving these animals on the ark, God had brought about their extinction for his own purposes. This idea of divinely inspired extinction seemed more acceptable, so it became fashionable to identify various unexplained fossils as remnants of creatures from the world before Noah. One common view, for instance, was that the mysterious large thighbone discovered in England in 1677 originally belonged to one of a race of giant people mentioned in the Bible.

Baron Georges Cuvier, the noted French anatomist who became the first major scientist to endorse the concept of natural extinction of species.

Opening the Debate on Extinction

By the late eighteenth century, however, increasing evidence pointed to the fact that extinction was a natural phenomenon and that forms of life different from those of the present had once existed. The first major scientist to champion the idea of natural extinction was French anatomist Baron Georges Cuvier (1769–1832). In 1796, at an important scientific conference, Cuvier announced his belief that extinctions had occurred regularly and frequently in the past. As

This extinct marine predator, Mosasaurus *(which was not a dinosaur), reach a length of up to twenty-five feet and inhabited the world's seas from about 150 to 65 million years ago.*

evidence, he cited the recent discovery of the fossil remains of a *Paleotherium*, a smaller version of modern horses. Because the *Paleotherium* no longer exists, said Cuvier, it must have become extinct. Cuvier also reported that elephant remains found beneath the streets of Paris were anatomically different than modern elephants native to Africa and India. So the Parisian elephant, he insisted, had also become extinct.

Cuvier was even more fascinated by the apparent existence of large extinct reptiles. In 1770, workers in a chalk quarry in the Netherlands had found a fossil set of jaws more than three feet long. When French soldiers brought the jaws to Paris in the 1790s, Cuvier examined them and immediately recognized that they belonged to a huge marine (sea-dwelling) reptile. A colleague later named the creature *Mosasaurus*. Because the *Mosasaurus* bore little resemblance to modern reptiles, Cuvier reasoned that it was a very ancient and extinct species. Not long afterward, he examined a fossil reptile that had been recently unearthed in Germany. To Cuvier's surprise, the fossil showed the remains of wings, although it clearly was not a bird. He named it *Pterodactyl*, meaning "wing finger," and declared that it had been a flying reptile that had lived in the remote past and then become extinct.

As determined by later scientists, neither the *Mosasaurus* nor the *Pterodactyl* were dinosaurs, so Cuvier was not the first to identify and name a dinosaur. However, his pioneering work in the identification of ancient species opened wide the scientific debate about extinction. Of some 150 fossil species found in the basin of France's Seine River, Cuvier demonstrated that 90 no longer existed. Moreover, his anatomic analyses of these remains were so complete and precise that many other scientists were compelled to agree with him, despite the fact that his view of extinction contradicted that of the Bible. Cuvier even supplied what many saw as a convincing cause for periodic extinctions—natural catastrophes. "Living things without number," he wrote,

> were swept out of existence by the catastrophes. Those inhabiting the dry lands were engulfed by deluges [floods]. Others whose home was in the waters perished when the sea bottom suddenly became dry land; whole races were extinguished leaving mere traces of their existence, which are now difficult of recognition, even by the naturalist.[6]

By showing that many animals, including large and exotic reptiles, had lived long ago and eventually died out, Cuvier had laid the groundwork for the discovery of a special class of ancient reptiles—the dinosaurs.

A New Class of Giant Land Reptiles

Indeed, the identification of dinosaurs became inevitable. Following Cuvier's work with fossils, searching for the remains of long-dead reptiles became a popular pastime in Europe, and many amateur finds became famous. One such find was that of a young English girl named Mary Anning, who discovered the skeleton of a thirty-foot-long marine monster. Scientists dubbed the creature *Ichthyosaurus*, or "fish lizard."

Then came Mary and Gideon Mantell's watershed discovery of a dinosaur tooth in 1822. Gideon Mantell subsequently

A long-necked Plesiosaurus *encounters a more massive* Ichthyosaurus *in a warm Mesozoic lagoon.*

dug up more teeth and bones belonging to the same kind of animal. He concluded that they were extremely old but was at first unable to identify them. So he showed them to the two most eminent anatomists of the day—Cuvier in Paris and William Buckland in Oxford, England. Mantell told them that the fossils had come from very old layers of rocks, but the two experts were unsure of his analysis. They suggested that the relics were more recent and constituted the remains of a known creature, perhaps a large fish or rhinoceros.

Mantell, however, stubbornly stuck to his original hypothesis—that the fossils were those of a very ancient and probably extinct creature. After further study, he noticed that the teeth closely resembled those of living South American iguana lizards, which are typically one to three feet long. The main difference was that the fossil teeth were much larger than those of modern iguanas. In 1825, Mantell published a description of what he called *Iguanodon*, or "iguana tooth." He claimed that the beast was an extinct land lizard that was about forty feet long and herbivorous. As reputable scientists do, Cuvier quickly and graciously admitted his previous error and accepted Mantell's conclusions.

However, later scientists determined that some of the details of Mantell's description of *Iguanodon* were incorrect. It was not, as he had assumed, a direct ancestor of modern iguana lizards. He also mistakenly envisioned the creature as walking on all fours like typical reptiles, and he thought its unusually large upright thumb bone was a horn that protruded from its head. Nevertheless, his estimate of the beast's size was essentially correct, as was his supposition that it was an herbivore. Most important, Mantell firmly established that large extinct reptiles had inhabited the land as well as the sea and air. He went on to discover another ancient land reptile in 1833. Called *Hylaeosaurus*, meaning "forest reptile," it was another herbivore, in this case with armor plating and large bony spines, like those of mythical dragons, running down its back.

In the meantime, William Buckland had identified his own extinct land reptile. In the mid-1820s, he described *Megalosaurus*, or "big reptile," as a carnivorous creature. After getting Cuvier's opinion about the animal's large thighbone, Buckland wrote:

> From these dimensions, as compared with the ordinary standard of the lizard family, a length exceeding 40 feet and a bulk equal to that of an elephant seven feet high [at the shoulder] have been assigned by Cuvier to the individual to which this bone belonged.[7]

The Changing of the Guard

In the following few years, an increasing number of ancient land reptiles and other prehistoric creatures came to light, and to deal with these discoveries, a whole new scientific field came into being. In 1838, renowned geologist Charles Lyell coined the term *paleontology*, from Greek words meaning "the science of ancient being," to describe the new discipline. Yet researchers in the field still had not effectively named and categorized the kinds of creatures they were studying. As late as 1840, for instance, they continued to lump all extinct reptiles together, ignoring huge differences in anatomy and the fact that some lived on land and others in the sea.

This situation frustrated the respected English anatomist Richard Owen. He had closely studied the remains of *Iguanodon*, *Megalosaurus*, and *Hylaeosaurus* and had concluded that they showed significant differences from other ancient reptiles. First, Owen pointed out, these three creatures were land rather than sea dwellers. Second, they were huge—much larger than any known modern land reptiles. Third, and most important, their pelvic bones and bellies were raised from the ground, so they walked upright, more like mammals than lizards, which tended to drag themselves along the ground. These special creatures, Owen believed, should have their

This nineteenth-century drawing of Iguanodon *and* Megalosaurus *fighting incorrectly shows both as quadrupeds (four-legged creatures). In reality, they were bipeds, that mainly walked upright on two legs.*

own separate classification. And in 1841, he invented one for them. He called them dinosaurs, from the Greek words *deinos*, meaning "terrible," and *sauros*, meaning "lizard" or "reptile." Owen concluded,

> From the size and form of the ribs, it is evident that the trunk was broader and deeper in proportion than in modern Saurians [lizards], and it was doubtless raised from the ground upon extremities [limbs] proportionally larger and especially longer, so that the general aspect of the living Megalosaur must have proportionally resembled that of the large [mammals] which now tread the earth, and the place [in nature] of which seems to have been supplied [in past ages] by the great reptiles of the extinct Dinosauria order. [8]

In the year Owen gave the dinosaurs their name, Cuvier had been dead for nine years; Mantell was fifty-one, and Buckland fifty-seven. The old guard of fossil experts was passing, and Owen's colorful naming and descriptions of the "terrible lizards" captured the imagination of a new and eager generation of fossil hunters and adventurers. These scientists began their careers in an era when the first great mystery about the dinosaurs had been solved. Extinction had proven to be a real and crucial natural process, and dinosaurs had been shown to be extinct creatures that had once ruled the earth.

A Second and Bigger Mystery

But the paleontologists and geologists still had their work cut out for them. A second and even bigger mystery—what killed the dinosaurs?—had not yet begun to be explored in any detail. Most of the old guard showed remarkably little interest in the reasons for the great late Mesozoic extinction, and most of those who did address the issue assumed, as Cuvier had, that some unidentified catastrophe had been the culprit. Part of the reason for this attitude was undoubtedly the rather limited state of the methods, instruments, and overall knowledge of paleontologists and geologists at the time. Unfortunately, such limitations made it exceedingly difficult to unearth and interpret any convincing evidence for such catastrophes or other possible reasons for the extinction. So it would fall to new generations of researchers to begin uncovering such evidence and mount determined efforts to solve the greatest dinosaur mystery of all.

Chapter 2

Initial Explanations for the Dinosaurs' Demise

When scientists began attempting to solve the mystery of the death of the dinosaurs, it struck them how sudden and wide-ranging the Mesozoic extinction had been. This seemed strange because it appeared to contradict the normal pattern of extinction, which evidence showed occurs in nature on a fairly regular basis. In fact, far more species have become extinct than exist on earth today. As a rule, though, various species belonging to a related group tend to die off gradually, leaving the group as a whole intact. Bird species such as the giant moa, the dodo, and the passenger pigeon became extinct, for example, but most other types of birds are still around.

By contrast, *all* of the dinosaurs—every species in every corner of the globe—appeared to have died at about the same time and relatively abruptly (within a few thousand or million years, which is abrupt in geological terms). Scientists were able to determine this by studying fossils of living things lying in the strata, or layers, of earth and rock deposited over millions of years. According to the dating scheme created by these experts, the mass dying in which the dinosaurs perished ended the Cretaceous period, the last of the three periods making up the Mesozoic era. (The three Mesozoic periods were the Triassic, lasting from 225 to 200 million years ago; the Jurassic, 200 to 135 million years ago; and the Cretaceous, 135 to 65 million years ago.) Scientists call the period following the Cretaceous the Tertiary, in which mammals inherited the earth. The physical division between the two periods, as it appears in the geological strata, is referred to as the Cretaceous-Tertiary, or K-T, boundary. (The letter *K*, which stands for *Kreide*, the German word for Cretaceous, is used to avoid confusion with the earlier Cambrian period.) Because no dinosaur fossils have ever been found in strata above the K-T boundary, scientists concluded that these creatures had all died completely and relatively suddenly; moreover, a common cause for all, or at least most, of these deaths seemed likely. In the words of noted zoologist David Norman,

The tip of the pick seen in this photo, taken at Drumheller, in Alberta, Canada, points to the narrow but crucial K-T boundary, marking the time of the dinosaurs' demise.

The simultaneous extinction of a whole range of species, both closely and distantly related, implies that some common cause or event must have been responsible. The possibility that all the [dinosaur] species went extinct purely coincidentally seems too remote for most scientists to give it serious consideration.[9]

As researchers continued to study and interpret the K-T boundary over the years, a number of them began to propose theories to explain this "simultaneous extinction" that ended the dinosaurs' long reign. A total of about eighty such proposals have been issued to date, the largest number appearing between 1920 and 1970. The proposals can be conveniently divided into general groups with common themes, such as biological disadvantages and ailments, changes in vegetation, climatic and geological changes, extraterrestrial explanations (those originating from beyond the earth), and so forth.

Before the 1990s, the scientific community never rallied around and accepted any one of these theories, although some were more popular than others with a majority of researchers. The main problem was that no single proposal seemed to account for the death of so many and diverse species inhabiting every continent and sea. Along with the dinosaurs, all of the flying reptiles had disappeared, as had about 40 percent of all marine animals, at least a third of all land mammals, and large numbers of amphibian, reptilian, and plant species. Not surprisingly, therefore, each new theory that came along found itself under fire from some quarter of the scientific community.

Egg Stealers and Tiny Brains

Some of the first attempts to explain the extinction of the dinosaurs invoked biological disadvantages or ailments as the agents of mass death. One theory proposed in the late nineteenth century suggested that rodentlike mammals crept into the dinosaurs' nests and devoured the eggs. Supposedly, the huge reptiles were at a disadvantage because they had to

spend much of their time searching for food, which left their eggs unguarded and exposed to attack by the quicker, smarter mammals. Eventually, the dinosaurs could not lay new eggs quickly enough to replenish their losses and extinction ensued.

The remains of a nest of Protoceratops *(beaked dinosaurs) eggs unearthed in the twentieth century.*

That this idea remained popular well into the twentieth century is perhaps attributable to species bias on the part of the mammalian investigators. The image of crafty warm-blooded mammals outwitting and defeating their monstrous, cold-blooded enemies and thereby clearing the way for the rise of humankind certainly appeals to the warm-blooded human ego. However, a few moments' reflection, as Norman points out, are probably all that is needed to come to a decision about this particular theory. In the first place, it is exceedingly improbable that the change to an egg-eating diet by mammals should have caused the extinction of *all* dinosaur species; after all, we cannot even be sure that all had eggs! Secondly, many egg-eating species are known today but these show no sign whatever of causing the extinction of their prey; indeed, it is biological "common sense" not to cause the extinction of the organisms that you feed upon. Otherwise, you will surely hasten your own end![10]

A reconstruction of two specimens of the carnivorous, human-sized dinosaur Deinonychus, *meaning "terrible claw."*

Another serious weakness of the egg-eating hypothesis was that it did not explain the huge scope of the K-T extinction. Clearly, mammalian consumption of dinosaur eggs cannot account for the extinction of sea creatures and plants, not to mention other mammals.

Another long-popular biological theory claimed that the dinosaurs died out because their brains were too small. According to this view, proposed by Belgian paleontologist Louis Dollo, as the dinosaurs' bodies grew increasingly larger, their brains stayed the same size. The *Apatosaurus* (originally called *Brontosaurus*), a huge plant eater with a long neck and tail, seemed a perfect illustration of this notion. The beast weighed up to thirty tons or more, yet its brain was only about the size of an orange. Dollo and other experts suggested that such a small brain could no longer efficiently control such a giant body or that the animal became, in effect, too "stupid" to adapt to normal environmental changes, so it died out along with the rest of the dim-witted dinosaurs.

This thesis, however, like the egg-eating one, was eventually shown to be faulty. A number of scientists pointed out that large dinosaurs had managed to survive with small brains for some 160 million years without any apparent threat to their survival. Furthermore, not all dinosaurs were huge and stupid. Some, such as the carnivorous *Velociraptor* and *Deinonychus*, were about the size of a human (and others were the size of chickens), and their brains were relatively large in relation to their body weight. In addition, it appears that they were clever, successful hunters and that they stalked their prey in packs, a kind of activity that requires group coordination abilities seen only in intelligent creatures. Finally, the small-brain proposal, like the egg-eating theory, failed to explain the wide range of extinctions at the K-T boundary. Dinosaurian stupidity obviously would have posed no threat to sea animals, mammals, and plants.

Senility and Disease

One of the more unorthodox biological arguments for the dinosaurs' demise advanced the notion of "racial senility," the idea that the "race," or general biological group, to which the various dinosaur species belonged grew too old and died. "Earlier generations of scientists," John Wilford explains, believed that a race of animals, like the life of an individual, goes through stages of growth and decline. It has its youth, its period of adaptation and maturation, its more settled middle age, and finally, its period of senility. And so, toward the end of the Cretaceous, senility must have come to the dinosaurs.[11]

The evidence cited by this theory's proponents was that many species of dinosaur eventually seemed to develop oversized, abnormal, and/or useless physical features, especially on their skulls. The armor-plated *Triceratops*, which walked on all fours, for example, had a huge bony frill running along the back of its head and neck, and *Pachycephalosaurus*, an herbivore that walked on its hind feet, sported a thick dome of solid bone on the top of its head. These features served no useful purpose, the argument went, and therefore they must be part of the series of natural physical malfunctions that inevitably accompanies "old age."

Later researchers showed that unusually large bony frills and skulls served to protect the animals' sensory organs or to support their large and active jaw muscles. Thus, these features were actually evidence of continuing adaptability and success rather than racial old age and failure. In addition, critics pointed out, many animal species, including sharks, horseshoe crabs, and cockroaches, to name only a few, existed in the age of the dinosaurs and are still alive and thriving. If racial senility is a fact of life, these species should be extinct, too.

Disease was still another suggested biological cause for the great dinosaur extinction. In one version of this theory, a deadly plague developed and steadily spread throughout the dinosaurian population, eventually wiping out all its members. Another version holds that dinosaur species from one continent migrated to other continents, and the natural germs the travelers carried infected and destroyed indigenous dinosaur species. "Every species of reptile, bird, and mammal carries its own unique load of parasites and disease organisms," writes noted paleontologist Robert Bakker.

And many foreign organisms will find no native enemy to hold them in check, so they will run amok. All the worst outbreaks of disease that have swept through mankind or its domestic stock have ultimately come from the introduction of foreign species. . . . The late Cretaceous world contained all the prerequisites for this kind of disaster. . . . A monumental immigration of Asian dinosaurs streamed into North America, while an equally grand migration of North American fauna moved into Asia. In every region touched by this global intermixture, disasters large and small would occur. A foreign predator might . . . suddenly disappear, the victim of a disease for which it had no immunity. As species intermixed from all corners of the globe, the result could only have been global biogeographical chaos.[12]

The main objection to this theory was that disease is usually very selective in its attacks. Some diseases affect only

This skeleton of a Triceratops *(meaning "three-horned face") shows the creature's famous horns and bony neck frill.*

humans, for example; others affect only certain kinds of animals or plants. Science has never observed a single disease or group of related diseases that is lethal to most animals as well as many plants. However, only such a "superbug" that could kill dinosaurs, marine creatures, mammals, and plants alike could account for the wide scope of the K-T extinctions. Moreover, "it is quite difficult to kill off even all of a single species with disease," Gregory Paul points out.

> The resistant individuals that almost invariably survive are well-positioned to make a comeback. Over the last half-millennium, mortality rates among various [local] human and animal populations have often exceeded 90 percent, but no species has yet gone extinct, and full recoveries have often occurred. Killing off even a fraction of the dozens or hundreds of dinosaur species via this mode may well be impossible. Besides, birds had been flying across and between the continents and spreading disease among themselves . . . for tens of millions of years without disastrous results.[13]

Unfamiliar and Poisonous Plants

Changes in vegetation were also frequently cited as possible mechanisms for killing off the dinosaurs. For example, University of Chicago scholar Van Valen proposed that the habitats in which most dinosaurs lived grew colder, causing the subtropical plants the herbivorous dinosaurs were used to eating to be replaced by plants that grow in more temperate zones. Put simply, the dinosaurs could not stomach this new kind of food and eventually starved to death. In turn, the carnivorous dinosaurs, such as the huge *Tyrannosaurus rex*, survived by eating the herbivores, so if the plant eaters died out, the meat eaters would quickly follow.

The first objection to this theory was that not all plants in a given region are replaced when temperatures shift. Furthermore, the older ones that remain will continue to nour-

A Stegosaurus, *an herbivore with bony plates running down its back, encounters a large carnivore. If the herbivores had starved to death, some theories logically proposed, the carnivores would soon have followed.*

ish at least some of the native species. One exception would be those species that eat only one or two kinds of plants, but evidence suggests that most dinosaurs were not such selective eaters. Also, such changes in vegetation over large regions occur extremely slowly, so dinosaurs should have had ample time to migrate to subtropical regions or otherwise adapt. Noted geologist Kenneth Hsü sums up these objections:

Although there may have been some dinosaur species that ate only one sort of sago palm or one brand of fern, the tribe as a whole ate everything in sight. They were everything from wood chewers to grasshopper catchers, conifer browsers to possum hunters. Furthermore, herds tend to move to where their fodder is, as predators follow their prey. If the zone of subtropical plants did shift southward, why didn't dinosaurs follow them? Such "movement" —a shift in population really—is measured in feet per year [so the dinosaurs could easily have followed the subtropical plants as they receded toward warmer regions].[14]

Chalk deposits and lush vegetation dominate this reconstructed Cretaceous landscape. If subtropical plants had shifted southward, herbivorous dinosaurs would have moved with them.

In addition, recent research has revealed that dinosaurs flourished in all kinds of environments and temperatures, some of them in temperate zones and a few even in subarctic habitats with cool temperatures and sparse vegetation. This shows that at least some of the creatures could easily have adapted to regional changes in vegetation and survived.

Another way that changes in vegetation might have killed the dinosaurs, London-based scientist Anthony Swain proposed, was by poisoning them. During the middle of the Cretaceous period, Swain pointed out, flowering plants developed and spread across the landscape. Unlike the conifers and ferns the dinosaurs were used to, flowering plants contain fair amounts of alkaloids, chemicals that are bitter tasting and can be lethal to animals in large doses. Swain argued, then, that the dinosaurs died out from alkaloid overdoses.

The poisoned-plant hypothesis "was a good story," says Hsü, but when scrutinized closely it had too many holes in it to be taken seriously. "Even if Swain was correct in all his speculations," Hsü adds,

> he only explained the demise of herbivorous dinosaurs. Who "murdered" the tyrannosaurs? How did he explain the delayed reaction, for the dinosaurs died out many millions of years after the rise of flowering plants? Swain had anyhow ignored the variety of reptiles, marine invertebrates, mammals, birds, and even quite a few flowering plants that also became extinct at that time. [15]

Cold Weather and Drifting Continents

Among some more popular proposals for the great dinosaur extinction were certain large-scale climatic and geological changes. These theories held that the extinction began millions of years before the period delineated by the K-T boundary and was fairly gradual. Thus, the K-T boundary marked the death not of all the dinosaurs but of the last survivors of a dying breed.

The most prevalent climatic theory, suggested that large portions of the earth's landmasses cooled off dramatically in the last part of the Cretaceous period. The change not only caused changes in vegetation that adversely affected the dinosaurs' diet but made it too cold for the creatures to survive. This idea was based largely on the supposition that dinosaurs, like other reptiles, were cold-blooded animals that could not produce their own internal body heat, as mammals do. In that case, the dinosaurs would have relied instead on direct sunlight and warm tropical air to keep them warm, and they were simply unable to cope with the cooling trend.

What could have caused such a major shift in climate? Some scientists suggested that continental drift was to blame. Evidence shows that all the present continents were once part of one huge landmass, which geologists dubbed Pangaea. This supercontinent began to break up about 190 million years ago (during the early Jurassic period) and, as Norman explains, by the late Cretaceous period,

> continental movement had separated all the major continents. . . . [This ongoing] activity may have resulted in appreciably raised sea-levels . . . resulting in shallow seas dividing, for example, west from east North America, Asia from Europe, and subdividing Africa. The effect of all these separate continental areas may have been to alter ocean current, wind patterns, and consequently climatic patterns from the prevailing mild conditions of the Jurassic and early Cretaceous to the cooler, more seasonal conditions which seem to mark the late Cretaceous.[16]

Whether or not the breakup of Pangaea and subsequent spread of the continents was the primary cause of climatic change in the Mesozoic era, the idea that such change killed all the dinosaurs remains doubtful. The fact is that major climatic change occurred throughout that era, even while dinosaurs were increasing in diversity, spreading far and wide, and becoming the masters of the earth. Moreover, Paul points out, during these years

> there was no onset of an ice age, or long-term superheating that left even the poles hot in the winter. For that matter, Mesozoic climates were not quite as universally warm and balmy as is usually thought. Winters

were probably quite chilly in continental interiors, and there may have been even modest continental glaciation [formation of glaciers] at the south pole. Dinosaurs and birds had long been living and reproducing in climates ranging from polar to tropical, wet forests to desert. . . . They appear to have had well-developed thermoregulatory systems [i.e., ways of regulating their internal temperature; in fact, many scientists have come to believe that most dinosaurs were warm-blooded like mammals]. Dinosaurs had the option of moving if changing climate in a particular location became a problem. Climatic change appears ill-suited to explain the entire collapse of the Dinosauria.[17]

This illustration shows one of several proposed shapes for the original supercontinent of Pangaea. Some scientists thought that Pangaea's breakup caused climatic changes with which the dinosaurs could not cope.

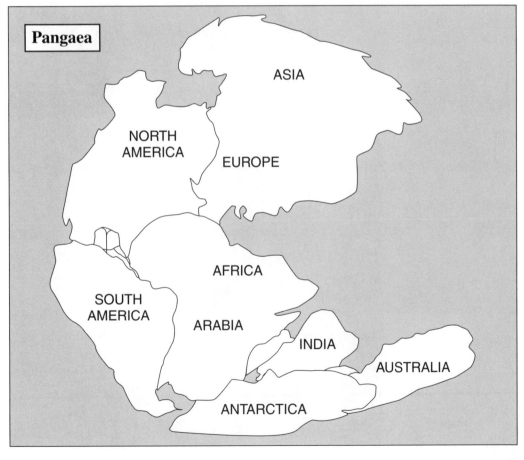

Exploding Stars and Cosmic Dust

In addition to the numerous biological, climatic, and other earthly explanations for the death of the dinosaurs, a few scientists eventually resorted to *un*earthly explanations. The first such suggestion came from a leading Russian astronomer, Joseph Shlovsky, in 1956. Shlovsky proposed that the dangerous effects of a supernova might be the culprit in the dinosaur murder mystery. One of the most destructive events in all of nature, a supernova is essentially an exploding star. When a star that is several times the size of the sun becomes unstable, it can explode, releasing an enormous blast of energy in the form of light, heat, and powerful radioactive particles.

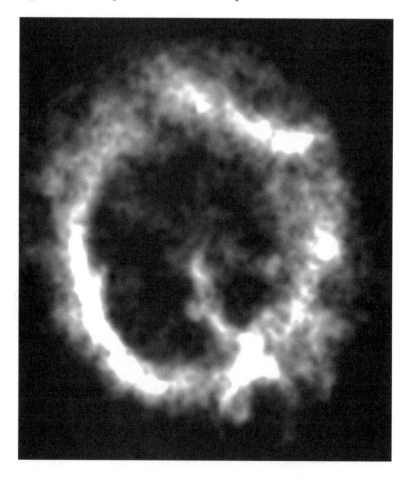

An image made by the Chandra X-ray Observatory in 1999 shows the gaseous remnants of an exploded star. Such a supernova was at one time a proposed candidate for the great dinosaur extinction.

If a nearby star had gone supernova about 65 million years ago, Shlovsky reasoned, it would have showered the earth with lethal radiation. Many creatures would have died immediately; others would have died a few years later from cancer or lost their ability to reproduce. Such a disaster would also have destroyed many plant species, and it might even have affected the climate. The reason some mammals and other small creatures survived, Shlovsky said, was that they burrowed underground where layers of dirt protected them from the radiation. In the meantime, some crocodiles and turtles buried themselves in mud, so their species also survived. Dinosaurs, by contrast, had no place to hide, so they succumbed to the catastrophe.

The supernova theory, which American scientists Dale Russell and Wallace Tucker elaborated on in a controversial 1971 article in the journal *Nature*, seemed to explain many aspects of the K-T extinction quite satisfactorily. However, most of Russell's and Tucker's colleagues were not convinced. They pointed out that such a disaster would leave "fingerprints," or physical evidence, in the rocks of the earth's crust. In particular, they said, a nearby supernova would leave traces of radioactive elements, such as plutonium, in the rocks. Even if randomly distributed and moved around by natural forces over the millennia, these traces would be fairly easy to detect with modern equipment. However, researchers found no traces of plutonium in the rock and clay layers around the K-T boundary, which seemed to rule out the supernova hypothesis.

A supernova was not the only extraterrestrial explanation advanced to account for the dinosaurs' demise. Scientists Michael Rampino and Richard Stothers, both of the Goddard Institute for Space Studies in Maryland, suggested that about 65 million years ago the earth passed through a large cloud of cosmic dust. The dust temporarily blocked a large proportion of sunlight from reaching the earth's surface, lowering temperatures and causing many plants to die. This would have negatively affected both the dinosaurs' body temperatures and their food supplies.

Still another extraterrestrial agent was proposed in 1973 by Nobel Prize–winning scientist Harold Urey. Though Urey did not pretend to have any solid evidence, he tentatively suggested that a large comet or meteorite might have struck the earth, suddenly and sharply raising global temperatures. As might be expected, Urey's admitted lack of evidence was enough to make most scientists reject the theory outright. Without some kind of clear, compelling evidence, these scientists said, the idea was just another interesting bit of speculation. It would not remain mere speculation for long, however. Unbeknownst to all involved, the discovery of the compelling evidence for a cosmic intruder causing the extinction of the dinosaurs was only six years away.

Chapter 3

Clues to Cosmic Collision

By the mid-1970s, the death of the dinosaurs was still as large a mystery as it had ever been. The wide and somewhat bewildering array of potential causes that had been proposed over the years to explain the great extinction had only served to underscore the fact that no single explanation satisfied a majority of experts. Yet most paleontologists, geologists, and other scientists who studied dinosaurs seemed more or less undisturbed by this state of affairs. After more than a century of fruitless debate, the prevailing attitude seemed to be that the scientific community was never going to reach any sort of overall agreement on the matter. There simply was not enough compelling, irrefutable evidence for any one theory to convince everyone. And in any case, scientists wondered, did it really matter all that much if no definitive solution to the mystery could be found? The late, respected paleontologist Tom Schopf, of the University of Chicago, summed up the attitude of most of his colleagues when he said:

> A satisfactory explanation of the cause of the extinction of the dinosaurs has been known for some years. . . . Probably more than 99.99999% of all the species that have ever existed on earth are now extinct. . . . The dinosaurs are among these. Extinction is the normal way of life. . . . As far as is currently known, it does not seem necessary to invoke an unusual event to account for the demise of the dinosaurs.[18]

Furthermore, the prevailing attitude was that even if some cause were eventually found for the dinosaurs' demise, that cause would likely not be very sudden and catastrophic in nature. By this time, the vast majority of scientists had come to believe that sudden global-scale disasters were extremely rare or even nonexistent; rather, the scientists thought, natural processes such as changes in the earth's surface and the evolution and extinction of life happened more gradually. According to this view, although the dinosaurs had disappeared fairly quickly in geological terms, it had still taken at least a few million years. So any extraterrestrial theories, such as supernovas and asteroid impacts, which proposed huge, sudden catastrophes, were summarily dismissed by all but a scant few members of the scientific community. This attitude was about to change rather dramatically, however.

In the mid-1970s, geologist Walter Alvarez and some colleagues made a strange and exciting discovery while examining some exposed strata of rock and clay at Gubbio, a small town in the Apennine Mountains north of Rome, Italy. That discovery soon proved to be the first in a series of tantalizing clues to a definitive solution for the great dinosaur mystery. Alvarez, along with his father, Nobel Prize–winning physicist Luis Alvarez, and other scientists, came to believe that the dinosaurs' killer was indeed extraterrestrial in origin. In their view, Harold Urey's 1973 educated guess—that the catastrophic impact of an asteroid had caused the great late Mesozoic extinction—had been right.

An Unexpected Discovery

Ironically, when Walter Alvarez and his colleagues found the first of these clues to cosmic collision, they were not studying the topic of dinosaur extinction at all. Instead, they were examining the rock layers at Gubbio to find evidence of reversals of the earth's magnetic field. As explained by James Powell, such reversals are

The late, great physicist, Luis Alvarez (left) and his son, geologist Walter Alvarez, examine an iridium sample discovered by Walter's team at Gubbio, Italy, in the mid-1970s.

times at which the north pole of the earth had acted as a south pole, and vice versa. . . . Geologists had discovered that, for reasons unknown, magnetic reversals were frequent (on their time scale), occurring on the average about every 500,000 years. Because all rocks of a certain age, wherever found, show the same magnetism—either normal (defined as the situation today) or reversed—we know that the reversals affected the entire earth at once.[19]

Alvarez and the other geologists were attempting to determine the exact pattern of magnetic reversals in the exposed strata at Gubbio so that they could create a more precise method of dating ancient rocks. The last thing on their minds at that time was the subject of dinosaurs; however, as many researchers know, sometimes a scientific discovery made in one field unexpectedly raises questions in another field, questions that send researchers scrambling to find answers.

The researchers at Gubbio encountered their first unexpected question when they examined the exposed K-T boundary layer in the gorge in which they were working. They noticed that the white limestone below the boundary was filled with the tiny fossils of an ancient variety of plankton, a one-celled organism that lives in the upper levels of the earth's oceans. The variety in question, foraminifera, is usually referred to as "forams" for short. Clearly, these forams thrived in the warm seas that covered the area in the late Cretaceous period. Alvarez and the others were puzzled, however, when they examined the layer of red limestone lying directly above the K-T boundary. This upper layer contained absolutely none of the forams so plentiful in the lower layer. Instead, the upper layer showed traces of a much rarer and smaller variety of foram. Stranger still, right at the boundary itself, separating the white and red limestone layers, the scientists found a one-centimeter-thick layer of reddish clay that contained no fossils at all.

Alvarez and his companions tried to make sense of what they had found. First, the older, more plentiful forams appeared to have disappeared rather abruptly at the K-T boundary, that is, about 65 million years ago. Then, as indicated by the thin layer of clay, for an undetermined period the ocean in that region was devoid (or at least nearly so) of forams. Finally, the upper limestone layer revealed that over time a new kind of foram developed and began to leave behind fossils.

The crucial question was exactly how long was the "undetermined period" during which the thin layer of clay had been deposited? Alvarez estimated that it was a few thousand years or less, a mere instant on geological time scales. If this were indeed the case, it would mean that the mass extinction that had killed the ocean forams and other sea life had happened with incredible suddenness. Moreover, and even more significant, the K-T boundary was already known to be the approximate marker ending the age of the dinosaurs. Considering all of these factors, Alvarez could not escape the suspicion that the evidence found at Gubbio pointed to an extremely abrupt and likely catastrophic cause for the great mass extinction. "What had happened to cause that extinction?" he later recalled asking himself.

And why was it so abrupt? At Gubbio, and in each new outcrop we found, there was a layer of clay about a centimeter thick, lacking fossils. . . . Did the clay have something to do with the extinction? The extinction of the marine microfossils that marked the K-T boundary in the Gubbio limestones was at least approximately the same age as the most famous of all extinctions— the disappearance of the dinosaurs. The more I thought about the K-T boundary, the more it fascinated me. . . . The disappearance of the Cretaceous forams as recorded in the [Gubbio] limestones appeared to have taken place suddenly, perhaps even catastrophically. But in the mid-1970s, the thought of

The K-T boundary is visible as a thin, light-colored horizontal strip in this photo taken near Trinidad, Colorado. Eventually, scientists found traces of iridium at the K-T boundary at sites around the world.

a catastrophic event in earth history was disturbing. As a geology student I had learned that catastrophism is unscientific. I had seen how useful the gradualistic view had been to geologists reading the record of earth history. . . . But nature seemed to be showing us something quite different. That little bed of clay at Gubbio was in conflict with gradualism, the most useful and cherished concept in geology.[20]

Luis Alvarez was fascinated by the evidence gathered at Gubbio by his son and became one of the chief scientific advocates of the K-T impact theory.

Traces of a Rare Metal Tell a Tale

Walter Alvarez was so intrigued by these findings that he decided to enlist his father, Luis, one of the world's greatest physicists, in trying to solve the mystery. After seeing a sample

of the rock layers from Gubbio, Luis Alvarez agreed that the initial key to unlocking the mystery was to determine more precisely the amount of time the layer of clay at the K-T boundary had taken to form. But how could this be done? Existing geological techniques for dating ancient rocks, clays, and fossils gave readings that were accurate to within a few million years; however, these techniques were not sensitive enough to measure time spans of a mere thousand years or less.

To overcome this limitation, the elder Alvarez suggested a new dating technique. It was based on the accumulation of traces of a rare metallic element called iridium in the clay. Powell explains why Alvarez chose iridium to help in dating the Gubbio clay:

When the earth formed, iridium, like other elements of the platinum group (which includes osmium, palladium, rhodium, and ruthenium), accompanied iron [another heavy element] into the [earth's] molten core, leaving these elements so rare in the earth's crust that we call some of them precious. Their abundance in meteorites and in the average material of the solar system is many times higher than in the earth's crust. The iridium found in sedimentary rocks (and often it is too scarce to be detected) appears to have settled from space in a steady rain of microscopic fragments—a kind of cosmic dust—worn from tiny meteorites that form the shooting stars that flame out high above the earth. Such meteorites are believed to reach the upper atmosphere at a constant rate, so that the metallic rain falls steadily to the earth, where it joins with terrestrial material. . . to settle to the bottom of the sea. There it is absorbed into the muds that accumulate on the seafloor and that eventually harden into rock. . . . The rate at which meteorites fall on the earth is known, as is the amount of iridium in meteorites.[21]

Iridium from space therefore accumulates on the earth's surface at a more or less given rate. Thus, by measuring the amount of iridium in the K-T boundary clay, Luis Alvarez reasoned, it was theoretically possible to estimate how long that clay had taken to accumulate on the ancient ocean floor.

The problem was that measuring the extremely tiny amount of iridium the scientists expected to find in the Gubbio clay layer could not be done with standard chemical analysis. A special research nuclear reactor was needed for the job. Fortunately, the Alvarezes and their colleagues, nuclear chemists Frank Asaro and Helen Michel, had access to such a reactor at the University of California at Berkeley (with which all four were associated). The scientists sent samples of the Gubbio limestone and clay layers to Berkeley and soon found themselves astounded by the

A clay layer containing iridium runs diagonally through this photo. The fact that the K-T boundary clays contain unusually high levels of iridium alerted the Alvarezes to a possible ancient cosmic collision.

results. The limestone layers above and below the K-T boundary had very low levels of iridium, just as expected. However, the thin clay layer lying right at the boundary had a full thirty times more iridium in it than predicted.

The first logical question raised by these findings was whether the high concentrations of iridium in the clay were peculiar and isolated to the Gubbio region or whether they existed elsewhere on the planet. Searching for an answer, Walter Alvarez examined some exposed K-T boundary layers at a site south of Copenhagen, Denmark. Sure enough, when Asaro used the Berkeley reactor to measure the iridium levels in the sample, he found concentrations of the metal even higher than those in the Gubbio clay.

Death from Space?

The Alvarezes and their colleagues immediately realized the implications of these iridium "spikes" in the K-T boundary clays. They knew that iridium is very rare in the earth's crust but plentiful in meteorites and other extraterrestrial bodies. Therefore, such high concentrations of the metal in a single, thin clay layer suggested a large-scale and presumably sudden extraterrestrial cause for the mass extinction that ended the Mesozoic era. At first, the supernova theory advanced by Joseph Shlovsky, Dale Russell, and Wallace Tucker seemed a promising candidate. But when the Alvarezes examined the Italian and Danish boundary layers for traces of plutonium, the telltale fingerprint of a supernova, they found none.

As a result, the Alvarez team laid the supernova theory to rest and began to focus on the possibility that a giant impact event had killed the dinosaurs and many other late Cretaceous species. But this line of reasoning also seemed problematic at first. Walter Alvarez remembers that

as Dad, Frank, Helen, and I tried to make sense of the iridium anomaly, we sometimes talked about a giant impact, but could not understand why an impact would cause worldwide extinction. Of course the blast would wipe out the nearby fauna [animals], but farther away the animals would survive and would quickly repopulate the devastated area. Impact in the ocean would cause a giant tsunami [large wave], but such a

A monstrous tsunami (seismic sea wave), generated by the undersea landslides caused by the K-T impact, crashes ashore in what is now the southern United States.

tsunami would be confined to a single ocean, and the effects would not be worldwide. A supernova had seemed more reasonable because it would have bathed the entire earth in lethal radiation, thus explaining the global character of the extinction. But a supernova was out, and impact seemed to provide no global killing mechanism. For over a year we searched discussions [i.e., scientific articles and other literature] that always ended in frustration, and I would lie awake at night thinking, "There just *has* to be a connection between the extinction and the iridium. What can it possibly be?"[22]

Rakata, part of the remains of the volcano that formed the island of Krakatoa, in the Sundra Strait. Krakatoa's 1883 eruption was one of the largest in recorded history.

A tentative but seemingly believable answer to this question came in the summer of 1979. After studying and rejecting numerous possible killing mechanisms a giant impact

might have produced, Luis Alvarez pointed out that an impacting asteroid would have pulverized huge amounts of rock and earth into dust while it was gouging out a giant crater. Much of that dust might have been blasted into the upper layers of the atmosphere, where it could have blocked sunlight worldwide for weeks, months, or even years.

For an analogy, Alvarez pointed to the famous eruption of the volcano Krakatoa (on a small island near the southern coast of the larger Indonesian island of Java) in 1883. The volcano had sent enough ash into the atmosphere to cause brightly colored sunsets across the globe for several months after the eruption. This ash also had blocked enough sunlight to noticeably lower temperatures in some parts of the world for up to three years after the event. Luis Alvarez realized that the giant impact he and his colleagues suspected of bringing the Cretaceous period to a catastrophic close would have been many thousands of times larger than Krakatoa's eruption. "Scale the Krakatoa event up to the size of a giant impact," Walter Alvarez later wrote, "and there would be so much dust in the air that it would get dark all around the world. With no sunlight, plants would stop growing, the whole food chain would collapse, and the result would be a mass extinction."[23]

Making and Fulfilling Predictions

Convinced that they had uncovered the cause of the dinosaurs' demise, the Alvarezes published a groundbreaking article outlining their impact theory—"Extraterrestrial Cause for the Cretaceous-Tertiary Extinction"—in the prestigious journal *Science* in June 1980. However, the paper did not, as the authors had hoped it would, quickly convince a majority of scientists that such an impact had actually occurred. In fact, most scientists, especially paleontologists, greeted the impact scenario with a great deal of skepticism and criticism. Part of this reaction was no doubt the result of personal pride and the automatic tendency to protect one's own professional turf. As Walter Alvarez puts it, "many paleontologists . . . did not think a geologist, a physicist, and two nuclear chemists should be trespassing in someone else's area of science."[24]

Even the few leading paleontologists who welcomed the impact theory (Stephen Gould and David Raup prominent among them) were ready to subject it to close and merciless scrutiny. That is, after all, the way all major new scientific theories are—and indeed must be—treated. In science, certain stringent criteria must be met before a theory can be accepted by a majority of researchers. First, the theory must satisfactorily explain all or at least most of the observed facts. Second, and even more important, a sound theory will invariably predict new facts that are yet to be discovered; if and when those facts *are* discovered, the theory will gain strength and may eventually be accepted by the scientific community. In contrast, if some of the predictions are later shown to have other, more credible explanations, the theory will be falsified.

Therefore, for the scientific community to accept the notion that the collision of an asteroid or comet killed the dinosaurs, the impact scenario would have to make and fulfill a number of predictions. First, the effects of the impact would have to be seen worldwide at the K-T boundary. If the Italian and Danish sites turned out to be the only places with significant concentrations of iridium in the boundary clays, the theory would be falsified. As it turned out, however, scientists swiftly discovered similar iridium spikes at other locations. By 1981, only a year after the Alvarezes' article appeared in *Science*, the number of such sites had risen to thirty-six; by 1983, it had reached fifty; and by 1990, the total was ninety-five sites and still rising.

Another prediction the theory had to fulfill was that the clay boundary layer containing the iridium would be thin everywhere in the world. As Powell points out,

> The immediate effects of a giant impact take place in minutes or hours; the secondary ones may last for hundreds or at most a few thousand years. On a geologic time scale, even these are instantaneous. Thus the boundary layer will be thin everywhere except, perhaps, at sites closer to ground zero.[25]

This prediction was also fulfilled: Throughout the 1980s and '90s, researchers found a consistently thin boundary layer at site after site around the globe.

Another prediction that would need to be fulfilled to validate the impact theory was that, as time went on, unanticipated discoveries should be made and these finds would support rather than falsify the theory. This too happened, not once but several times. For example, a team of scientists from the University of Chicago began studying the Danish K-T clays in an effort to uncover various meteoric elements. Unexpectedly, they found a layer of soot at the boundary. Such soot layers were subsequently found at many other sites. Supporters of the impact scenario concluded that the soot was a by-product of global fires ignited by the tremendous heat effects of the impact.

Another unanticipated discovery was that of millions of small diamonds at, but never below or above, the K-T boundary at most of the sites. Diamonds require enormous pressure and/or heat to form and so are normally found deep underground. A number of scientists have concluded that the only way these diamonds could have formed at the earth's surface and also be concentrated solely in the K-T boundary layer would be for them to have crystallized within the monstrous, white-hot fireball that expanded outward in the seconds immediately following the impact.

The "Smoking Gun"

Perhaps the most important prediction of all, one that could either make or break the impact theory, was that the impacting object would have created a huge crater, either on land or on the ocean floor. That crater, therefore, would have to be found. Without this so-called "smoking gun" of the proposed catastrophe, the theory would remain mere conjecture, no matter how much secondary supporting evidence was found. Moreover, not just any large crater would do. The smoking gun of the K-T event would have to be a certain size, for instance. The Alvarezes and other scientists estimated that the impacting object was six to ten miles in diameter and traveling at many miles per second when it struck the earth. Rough calculations showed that the crater it formed would be somewhere around 100 to 120 miles (or perhaps more) in diameter. Also, the crater would be about 65 million years old, since that is the age of the K-T boundary and accompanying mass extinction.

During the 1980s, as the search for the crater continued, impact supporters pointed out several possible reasons why no crater with such specifications was immediately visible. First, if the crater had formed on land, its surface features may have eroded away or filled in with sediments over the course of millions of years, or it might be hidden under the thick ice-packs of Greenland or Antarctica. On the other hand, if the impact had occurred in the ocean, over the course of time the seas would likely have deposited sediments in and over it, making it difficult to find. Or the section of sea floor on which the crater rested might have moved under a nearby continent, completely destroying the crater. (The sea floors are slowly but constantly spreading outward from their centers as new rock wells up from beneath the earth's crust; when a given portion of the moving sea floor reaches a continental margin, it is subducted, or driven beneath, the continental mass, where extreme pressure and heat crush it.)

As it turned out, the crater created by the K-T impact was still intact, although considerably eroded, buried, and therefore difficult to detect. The first important clue to its location came in 1989. University of Arizona scientists Alan

Hildebrand and William Boynton discovered compelling evidence that huge tsunamis had swept over the coasts of what are now Mexico, Cuba, and the United States at about the time the K-T boundary formed. This seemed to suggest that a large object had plunged into the Caribbean Sea. Chemical

A large extraterrestrial object plunges into the Caribbean Sea, as envisioned by advocates of the K-T impact scenario.

61

Speculative reconstruction of the explosion caused by the K-T impact sends destructive waves of energy rippling through the atmosphere and sea.

analyses of Caribbean rocks made in 1990 also indicated a large Caribbean impact, probably near Mexico's Yucatan peninsula. Finally, in 1991 scientists from NASA's Ames Research Center and other investigators confirmed the existence of a large impact crater partially submerged in the shallow waters off the Yucatan coast. The clincher came when scientists collected samples from rocks located at various points around the site. Laboratory tests dated all of these samples to approximately 65 million years ago. Popular scholar and dinosaur expert Don Lessem wrote in 1992:

The most celebrated scientific detective quest of the decade has now produced a "smoking gun." The presumed dinosaur-killer is a crater 120 miles wide formed by an object from space six miles across slamming into the earth with an impact 10,000 times more powerful than the explosion that would be produced by setting off all the world's atomic weapons simultaneously. The crater has been dubbed Chicxulub. . . . In ancient Mayan [the language of the Native American people of the same name who once inhabited the Yucatan], Chicxulub means "tail of the devil."[26]

Since Chicxulub's discovery, scientists have conducted numerous and diverse analyses of the crater, as well as various kinds of ejecta (rocks, dust, crystals, and other materials ejected during the crater's formation) found at sites across North America. These tests have confirmed with a high degree of certainty that the crater formed from the impact of a large extraterrestrial object 65 million years ago. Moreover, it appears equally certain that this catastrophic event created the K-T boundary layer observed at sites worldwide. As Powell puts it,

> Chicxulub is the impact crater. This is no longer a fascinating speculation, but closely approaches the status of observational fact. Today, those who doubt that Chicxulub is the long-sought crater can be counted on one's fingers. Yes, a giant meteorite did strike the earth at the end of the Cretaceous.[27]

Of course, proving that a giant impact did occur 65 million years ago is not the same as proving that the event killed the dinosaurs. Perhaps, suggested the handful of remaining skeptics, the disaster severely reduced the dinosaur population but still left some survivors. And maybe some other killing mechanism—perhaps disease or

This dramatic recent painting depicts the K-T object smashing into the coastal margin of what is now the Yucatan Peninsula (in eastern Mexico).

climatic change—subsequently killed off the survivors. Thus, to make a convincing case that the K-T event was the sole cause of the dinosaurs' extinction, supporters of the impact theory had to go beyond merely proving that the catastrophe occurred. They had to discern the sequence and scope of the impact's effects and show specifically how these effects could have caused the mass death of so many varied species.

Chapter 4

Death from the Sky

In the decades since Walter and Luis Alvarez and their colleagues seriously proposed the impact theory for the great K-T mass extinction, researchers from many branches of science have studied and evaluated the impact scenario. Astronomers have lent their expertise to arguments about the properties and velocities of comets and asteroids and just how often such extraterrestrial bodies actually strike the earth. Geologists have scrutinized the rock and clay strata to determine the size and properties of the crater and the placement and composition of the debris the blast deposited across the globe. Physicists and nuclear scientists have analyzed a growing mountain of data and computer simulations in an attempt to determine the size and energy output of the blast and its immediate effects on the earth's environment. Climatologists, chemists, and other experts have studied the possible atmospheric and weather-related effects that occurred in the following weeks, months, and years. And paleontologists, biologists, and zoologists have investigated the possible scope and nature of the disaster's harmful effects on various forms of life, including the dinosaurs.

In general, the consensus of the majority of these researchers is that the catastrophe that sounded the death knell of the dinosaurs and many other Cretaceous species was not a simple or straightforward event. The initial, primary stage of the disaster—the impact itself—*was* relatively simple: It consisted basically of a large, swiftly moving object striking the ground. However, that sudden strike set in motion a complex chain of events and processes that occurred in the minutes, days, months, and years that followed. Each of these secondary events and processes apparently contained one or more killing mechanisms and constituted a disaster unto itself. It is probable that none of these disasters individually would have been lethal enough to cause a mass extinction so large, but acting together, they produced a catastrophe

A recent reconstruction of the impacting asteroid (or comet) that ended the Mesozoic era. Impact-theory supporters suggest that the initial explosion set in motion a long series of large-scale and lethal catastrophes.

of epic proportions. The more evidence and information about the K-T disaster that accumulates, the more likely it seems that the impact did indeed produce the mass extinction observed in the geologic and fossil record.

The Impact and Fireball

That evidence paints an awesome and frightening picture of the chain of events that shattered the late Cretaceous world. In the last hours and minutes before impact, the earth was teeming with life. A rich array of plants thrived on land and in the sea. And trillions of animals roamed the landmasses or swam in the seas, just as they had all their lives and as countless generations of their ancestors had. Some lounged on rocks, absorbing the warmth of the tropical sun; others foraged for food in forests, tall grasses, treetops, or shallow coastal waters; still others, less fortunate, became food for some stronger, faster creature.

None of these denizens of the globe's complex, intricately related, and fruitful ecosystems could have known that the instrument of their death was hurtling at them from the sky. The object was a comet or asteroid at least six miles (ten kilometers) in diameter. (Scientists are still not sure which kind of extraterrestrial body it was. A comet is essentially an aggregate mass of ice, rocks, and dust, while an asteroid is a chunk of metal and rock. But the exact identity is ultimately irrelevant; either one of these bodies would have produced the same impact effects.)

The intruder sped toward the earth at a velocity modern experts estimate at between twelve and forty-two miles per second. This is fairly normal for cosmic bodies. But in earthly and human terms, it is an almost incomprehensible velocity. Moreover, it imparts to such an object a stupendous potential energy should it suddenly strike another body. In this case, that stored-up energy was roughly equivalent to 100 million megatons (100,000,000,000,000 tons) of TNT, 5 billion

Two T-rexes *and a* Triceratops *are about to be swept away by the blast wave from the monstrous K-T event, as fragments of the explosion light up the sky.*

times larger than the force unleashed by the atomic bomb dropped on Hiroshima, Japan, in World War II. When the object ended its journey and struck the earth, that enormous stored energy would inevitably be released. As James Powell aptly puts it, "An almost irresistible force was about to meet an immovable object."[28]

In the final few seconds before impact, the cosmic missile plunged through the atmosphere and zeroed in on a spot near the northern coast of the Yucatan peninsula. Dinosaurs and other creatures who happened to live on that side of the planet would have seen a blinding flash of light as the object was transformed into a monstrous fireball of incandescent gas, which was rich in iridium from the destroyed cosmic body.

That rapidly expanding fireball, say Walter Alvarez and
Frank Asaro, would

propel material [from both the vaporized object and
the earth's crust] out of the atmosphere. The fireball
of an atmospheric nuclear explosion expands until it
reaches the same pressure as the surrounding atmosphere, then rises to an altitude where its density
matches that of the surrounding air. At that point,
usually about 6 miles high, the gas spreads laterally
[side-to-side] to form the head of the familiar mush-
room cloud. Computer models of explosions with
energies of 1,000 megatons . . . only 1/100,000 the

A T-rex *watches the swift
expansion of the K-T
impact fireball in the
distance. Within seconds,
the blast of heat from the
explosion will reach the
creature and literally broil
it in its tracks.*

energy of the K-T impact, have shown that the fireball never reaches pressure equilibrium with the surrounding atmosphere. Instead, as the fireball expands . . . its rise accelerates and the gas leaves the atmosphere at velocities fast enough to escape the earth's gravitational field. The fireball from an even greater asteroid impact would simply burst out the top of the atmosphere, carrying any entrained ejecta [debris] with it, sending the material into orbits that could carry it anywhere on earth.[29]

Giant Earthquakes and Sea Waves

While the fireball shot skyward, a powerful atmospheric pressure (or shock) wave expanded out in all directions from ground zero, leveling every tree and killing every living thing in a radius of at least a thousand miles and possibly as far as two thousand. At the same time, the impact gouged out a crater up to ten miles deep and more than a hundred miles in diameter. This created a shock wave within the ground, a giant earthquake measuring 12 or 13 on the Richter scale. The force of this quake was so large that it raised the ground in waves hundreds of feet high for a distance of a thousand or more miles from ground zero. Even far beyond this radius, dinosaurs and other animals were swept into the air and crushed by the pressure wave, ground waves, or both.

The huge shock of the impact and crater formation near the Yucatan also dislodged large portions of the Caribbean Sea floor. Resulting landslides displaced enormous amounts of water from that sea, setting in motion a giant tsunami that rolled outward at hundreds of miles per hour. As the western and northern portions of the wave neared the coasts of what are now Mexico and the southern United States, the wave reared up to a tremendous height, perhaps a thousand feet or more, and crashed onto the land. Onward and onward the towering wall of water rushed, crushing everything in its path

for many miles inland. While this was happening, the wave's eastern portion moved unimpeded into the Atlantic Ocean. A few hours later, now smaller but still hundreds of feet high, it struck the coasts of Africa and Europe with devastating effect. Meanwhile, far to the south, another section of the liquid monster continued on; in less than a day, the huge wave traveled through all the oceans, completely flooding every low-lying coastal region on earth.

A rendition of the Chicxulub crater a few years after its formation. Over eons, the effects of water, weather, shifting sediments, and other natural forces eroded and hid the crater.

The Onset of Impact Winter

Horrendous as they were, the effects of the pressure wave, earthquakes, and tsunamis proved but a foretaste of the death and devastation to come. The fireball had blasted a gigantic hole in the atmosphere above Mexico and sent many cubic miles of pulverized debris (intermixed with iridium) into trajectories around the globe. A small amount of this material was ejected into space, but most of it soon came hurtling back down, creating a startlingly brilliant and beautiful, but unfortunately quite deadly, worldwide meteor shower. "The individual globules were traveling so fast," says Powell, "that they ignited, producing a literal rain of fire. Over the entire globe, successively later the greater the distance from the target, the lower atmosphere burst into a wall of flame, igniting everything below."[30] A few minutes later, nearly every forest in the

A T-rex is startled by small rain of meteors in the distance. It is possible that the great K-T impact was preceded by smaller, less deadly showers of cosmic debris.

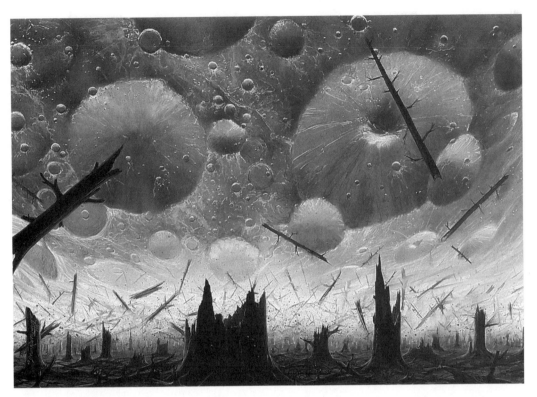

world was ablaze, and many of the still-living animals standing above ground were seared to death and then broiled as if in a giant oven. The soot created by these fires eventually fell back to earth, where millions of years later Walter Alvarez and other scientists found traces of it at the K-T boundary.

The smoke and soot from the global fires darkened the skies. But this was only temporary and of minimal impact compared to the artificial night that was already descending as a result of the dust thrown skyward by the impact itself. According to Alvarez and Asaro,

> Originally, we proposed that impact-generated dust caused global darkness that resulted in extinctions. According to computer simulations made in 1980 by Richard P. Turco of R&D Associates, O. Brian Toon of NASA, and their colleagues, dust lofted into the atmosphere by the impact of an object [like the one

A fanciful drawing depicts a forest being shattered by the massive atmospheric shock wave traveling in front of the asteroid (or comet) seconds before impact.

73

that caused the K-T event] would block so much light that for months you would literally be unable to see your hand in front of your face. Without sunlight, plant photosynthesis would stop. Food chains everywhere would collapse. The darkness would also produce extremely cold temperatures, a condition termed "impact winter." [Scientists have dubbed a similar but much smaller condition that might be caused by a nuclear war "nuclear winter."][31]

The breakdown of the food chain in an impact winter is fairly easy to understand and quite terrifying to contemplate. With temperatures plummeting to well below zero in most places and almost no sunlight getting through the dust-choked atmosphere, most of the vegetation spared by the fires quickly shriveled. Unable to find enough food, the remaining herbivorous dinosaurs died within a few days at most. Their death, in turn, doomed most of the carnivorous dinosaurs, which normally preyed on the plant eaters. Wandering blindly and fearfully through a darkened, burned-out, and now frozen landscape, the last surviving *Tyrannosaurus rex,* once the invincible king of the Cretaceous realm, crumpled helplessly to the ground, never to rise again.

Meanwhile, some of the smaller mammals that had for so long scattered and scampered to keep from being crushed beneath dinosaurian feet were, thanks to their fur, better able to adapt to the sudden cold. A number of mammals were used to living in underground burrows, and into these lairs they now retreated, venturing out now and then only long enough to snatch bits of nourishment from the millions of dinosaur carcasses littering the devastated continents. Some crocodiles, turtles, and other reptiles that could live for extended periods submerged in mud or river bottoms also survived.

Poison, Acid, and Abnormal Heat

Most of the plants and large land animals that might have managed to live for a while in the cold and dark probably eventually died from some very deadly secondary effects of the great impact and artificial winter. As Powell explains, poisonous vapors formed in the air, and the formation of other noxious compounds greatly prolonged the length of the unnatural night.

A surviving dinosaur finds itself marooned in an icy landscape created near one of the planet's poles by the sudden onset of impact winter.

The blast wave acted as a chemical catalyst, causing atoms of oxygen and nitrogen to combine to form various noxious compounds, many found in today's

smog. Sulfur oxides joined them, for in a coincidence unfortunate for life at the end of the Cretaceous, the Yucatan rocks at ground zero included sulfate deposits. . . . Sulfur dioxide formed tiny droplets that further obscured the sun and lowered temperatures even more. [Scientists] Kevin Pope, Kevin Baines, and Adriana Ocampo have calculated [in a 1997 article in the *Journal of Geophysical Research*] that the impact into the sulfur-rich deposits of the Yucatan would have produced over 200 billion tons of both sulfur dioxide and water, leading to a decade-long impact winter.[32]

Worse still, water droplets likely began to wash the nitrogen and sulfur compounds out of the air, setting in motion the next link in the ongoing chain of lethal events—acid rain. On the one hand, acid rain would have killed many of the remaining plants and animals (although acid-tolerating plants, small mammals, amphibians, and fish would have been little affected). On the other hand, the acid would have dispersed or dissolved some of the iridium and other blast debris that had already fallen to the ground. This would explain why layers of these elements are thin or nonexistent at a few of the sites examined by scientists. The toxic rain would also have significantly increased the acidity of the upper layers of the world's seas, killing much of the plankton, the normally abundant microscopic plants and animals that form the top of the ocean food chain. Severely reduced plankton levels would have caused the death of large numbers of fish and other small marine animals. This would explain why almost all the large carnivorous sea monsters, like the *Mosasaurus* and *Icthyosaurus*, which preyed on these smaller creatures, went extinct at this time.

Still another harmful process, one that may have occurred in the last stages of the catastrophe as the impact winter ended, was the so-called greenhouse effect. This occurs when water vapor (carbon dioxide or certain other gases) traps heat in the atmosphere, raising global temperatures to abnormal levels. A number of researchers, including University of Colorado scholar Eric Krause and the late Eugene Shoemaker of the U.S. Geological Survey, have suggested that an ocean impact like that of the K-T event would have

As the impact winter slowly begins to lift, a Triceratops *skull and a denuded, lifeless forest bear mute testimony to the devastating effects of the K-T impact.*

thrown large amounts of water vapor into the atmosphere. "The vapor, trapping the earth's heat," say Alvarez and Asaro,

> would stay aloft much longer than the dust, and so the impact winter would be followed by greenhouse warming. More recently, John D. O'Keefe and Thomas J. Aherns, of the California Institute of Technology, suggested that the impact might have occurred in a limestone area, releasing large volumes of carbon dioxide, another greenhouse gas. Many plants and animals that survived the extreme cold of the impact winter could well have been killed by a subsequent period of extreme heat.[33]

A Terminal Case of Bad Luck

This complex and lethal series of events, which began with the colossal impact and fireball and may have ended several years later with an extended period of greenhouse warming, devastated life on the planet. If the dinosaurs were among the casualties, as so many researchers believe they were, their long and successful reign as the earth's dominant life form ended dramatically. Indeed, it now seems highly likely that these magnificent and terrifying beasts met their doom in a cosmic catastrophe.

In a very real sense, then, paleontologist David Raup remarks, the dinosaurs suffered from a terminal case of bad luck. "Extinction," Raup writes,

> is evidently a combination of bad genes and bad luck. Some species die out because they cannot cope in their normal habitat or because superior competitors or predators push them out. But . . . I feel that most species die out because they are unlucky. They die because they are subjected to biological or physical stresses not anticipated in their prior evolution and because time is not available for . . . [them to] adapt.[34]

The flesh-eating Allosaurus, *an earlier relative to* T-rex, *remained king of its domain. Those of his descendants who walked the earth at the moment the K–T object struck were not so lucky.*

Put simply, the killer from the sky took the dinosaurs by surprise. After 160 million years of phenomenal success, their luck suddenly ran out, and when the darkness of that last, unnaturally long Cretaceous night finally lifted, all that was left was their bones.

Chapter 5

The Debate Continues

Despite the discovery of a considerable array of strong evidence supporting the impact theory as the cause of the mass extinction at the end of the Cretaceous period, a few experts remain unconvinced. This often frustrates pro-impact researchers. Before his death in 1988, Luis Alvarez expressed the frustration he felt with those colleagues, saying,

> I really cannot conceal my amazement that some paleontologists prefer to think that the dinosaurs, which had survived all sorts of severe environmental changes and flourished for 160 million years, would suddenly, and for no specified reason, disappear from the face of the earth . . . in a period measured in tens of thousands of years. I think that if I had spent most of my life studying these admirable and hardy creatures, I would have more respect for their tenacity and would argue that they could survive almost any trauma except the worst one that has ever been recorded on earth—the impact of the K-T asteroid.[35]

Despite this strongly worded statement and others aimed against them in the 1980s, the critics of the impact theory held their ground. Many of them changed their minds in the 1990s, however, with the verification of the size and age of the Chicxulub crater and other discoveries and studies. But a few skeptics continue to hold out, convinced that the pro-impact people have still failed to make their case. The impact critics, in general, though, no longer deny that the K-T impact occurred and caused widespread devastation. The evidence for this event is simply too overwhelming. As a result, the debate about it during the past two decades has convinced virtually all scientists that catastrophism can play a major role in environmental and biological change on earth.

What the critics remain unwilling to accept is that the K-T impact was the sole factor in the dinosaurs' demise. On the one hand, they say, some other kind of disaster, such as large-scale volcanism, could just as easily be responsible for the mass extinction. On the other, they point to the fact that the K-T biological catastrophe was not the only mass extinction that occurred in the past. Several other large extinction events occurred before the one at the close of the Cretaceous, they say, and so far no significant evidence has been found to suggest that any of them were caused by giant impacts. If these disasters can be explained by other means, their argument goes, these same means might well be used to explain the K-T extinction.

A group of plesiosaurs living near the Yucatan Peninsula are dazzled by the impacting asteroid (or comet) seconds before their demise.

Supervolcanism

In general, the impact critics believe that the K-T extinctions were a bit more gradual than the impact supporters claim. The vast majority of scientists now accept the existence of a layer of iridium deposited more or less world-wide and agree that it and other evidence point to a major catastrophe. However, the impact critics argue that the disaster that caused the extinction of the dinosaurs happened over the course of several thousand or a few million years, rather than in less than ten years as described in the impact scenario.

This longer time frame is consistent with today's chief alternative to the impact theory for explaining the K-T

A volcano spews out lava in a 1974 eruption. Some scientists believe that an episode of supervolcanism created the catastrophe that destroyed the dinosaurs.

extinctions—a large-scale episode of volcanism, often referred to as "supervolcanism." Ordinary volcanic eruptions, though sometimes very dangerous to humans and their habitations, are far too small in scope to account for a mass extinction. Even the simultaneous eruption of ten or twenty volcanoes in various parts of the world would be too small. But some evidence suggests that, on very rare occasions in the earth's history, a few unusually large episodes of volcanism have occurred. Supporters of this theory suggest that such catastrophes might produce many of the same effects noted in the impact scenario. For instance, a supervolcanic eruption might extract iridium from deep underground, where the element is more plentiful than in the earth's crust, and deposit it on the surface. Such an eruption (or more likely a series of eruptions) might also darken the sky for long periods, bringing on a "volcanic winter" and maybe even acid rain.

The first crucial question is whether there is any evidence of a volcanic episode on the scale needed to account for the K-T extinction. As early as 1972, Peter R. Vogt, a scientist at the Naval Research Laboratory in Washington, D.C., suggested that the Deccan Traps might constitute such evidence. Science had long known about the Deccan Traps, a group of enormous ancient lava flows covering much of western India. Geologists and volcanologists viewed them as solid evidence of a series of gigantic eruptions lasting, perhaps on and off, for several thousand or a few million years. But Vogt was the first researcher to connect the traps with the catastrophe that ended the Cretaceous period. Then, in the mid- to late 1970s, Dewey M. McLean, of the Virginia Polytechnic Institute, and Dartmouth College scholars Charles B. Officer and Charles L. Drake became serious supporters of the supervolcanism scenario. Today, Officer and Drake remain the theory's chief supporters and, not surprisingly, the chief critics of the impact theory.

Does the Theory Meet the Major Criteria?

To satisfactorily account for the death of the dinosaurs, supervolcanism must, of course, pass the same tests that impact supporters say their own theory has passed with flying colors. First, was the episode that formed the Deccan Traps truly large enough to cause a global catastrophe? Vincent Courtillot, a French geophysicist, thinks it was. "The sheer size of the Deccan Traps," he says,

> suggests that their formation must have been an important event in the earth's history. Individual lava flows extend well over 3,900 square miles and have a volume exceeding 2,400 cubic miles. The thickness of the flows averages from 33 to 164 feet and sometimes reaches almost 500 feet. In western India, the accumulation of lava flows is almost 8,000 feet thick (more than a quarter the height of Mount Everest). The flows may have originally covered more than 772,000 square miles, and the total volume may have exceeded 48,000 cubic miles. [36]

From these facts, Courtillot and other supervolcanism supporters conclude that the volcanic episode was hundreds of times larger than any eruption ever witnessed by humans.

Second, could the volcanic episode in question have produced many of the same disastrous effects attributed to the impact scenario? Again, Courtillot answers yes. He points out that scientists at NASA's Goddard Space Flight Center in Maryland used computers to model

> the manner in which fountains of lava, such as those from Kilauea in Hawaii, expel dust and ejecta. When scaled up to the dimensions of the Deccan volcanism, their models predict that large amounts of material should also be lofted into the atmosphere. Atmospheric circulation would distribute material rather evenly between the two hemispheres, no mat-

ter where it was originally emitted. . . . The first effect [of the eruption] would have been darkness resulting from large amounts of dust (volcanic ash) [blasted up] into the atmosphere. The darkness would have halted photosynthesis, causing food chains to collapse. . . . Life would also have been confronted by large-scale toxic acid rain [as sulfur released by the eruption turned to sulfuric acid in the air]. . . . [Another study] estimated that the Deccan Traps injected up to 30 trillion tons of carbon dioxide, six trillion tons of sulfur, and 60 billion tons of halogens (reactive elements such as chlorine and fluorine) into the lower atmosphere over a few hundred years.[37]

Kilauea, an active volcano on Hawaii, erupts in this recent photo. The eruption that created the Deccan Traps was undoubtedly hundreds of times larger.

A third important criterion the Deccan Traps have to meet is that their age must match that of the K-T boundary—65 million years. Supporters of the supervolcanism theory estimate that the episode that formed the traps occurred sometime between 64 and 68 million years ago. Though this is not an exact match, they say, the discrepancy "may be the result from alteration of the samples or differing laboratory standards."[38]

Are All Mass Extinctions Caused by Eruptions?

These scientists say that their argument is strengthened by the evidence for the other major mass extinctions detectable in the geological and fossil record. The list of these events, John Wilford explains,

> usually begins with the . . . pervasive [widespread] dying toward the end of Cambrian time, some half a billion [500 million] years ago. More than half of all

A fossilized trilobite. Many species of this marine creature with a segmented body died out during a mass extinction that occurred at the close of the Cambrian period.

animal species vanished then, including numerous species of trilobites [very plentiful marine creatures with outer shells and segmented bodies]. Another 30 percent of animal life, including many primitive fish, became extinct at the end of the Devonian [period], 360 million years ago. The most catastrophic extinction occurred 248 million years ago at the close of the Permian [period], when half of all animal families disappeared. Some 75 percent of the amphibians and all the surviving trilobites were wiped out. The toll was especially high among reptiles—an 80 percent loss—and this apparently cleared the field for the rise of the early dinosaurs. The dinosaurs somehow survived the next mass extinction, when most other reptiles died off 213 million years ago at the end of the Triassic [period]. Then came the Cretaceous calamity, the most recent of the really great extinctions.[39]

Some strong circumstantial evidence suggests that supervolcanism was involved in at least one of these mass extinctions—the largest one, the Permian. Even the staunchest impact supporter, Walter Alvarez, is impressed by what he calls a "strange coincidence." There is no evidence either for or against a giant impact 248 million years ago, the time of the Permian catastrophe, he says,

> because there is virtually no preserved stratigraphic record [surviving layers of strata] across the Permian-Triassic boundary anywhere in the world. On the other hand, the greatest of all outpourings of lava on the continents is the Siberian Traps, much like the Deccan Traps but substantially larger in volume. Recently Paul Renne at the Berkeley Geochronology Center has obtained reliable dates on both the Siberian Traps and Permian-Triassic boundary, and they are indistinguishable![40]

Based on this and other circumstantial evidence surrounding the formation of the Deccan Traps, Courtillot, Officer, Drake, and a few others theorize that most or all of the mass extinctions, including the K-T event, were caused by supervolcanism.

Critics of Supervolcanism

Though the supervolcanism theory remains a viable explanation for the K-T event and dinosaurs' demise, most scientists have not embraced it with the enthusiasm they have for the impact scenario. The impact supporters argue first that the dating and duration of the Deccan eruptions do not correspond with the evidence for the great extinction at the K-T boundary. According to James Powell, the newest dating tests, which were conducted by French and Indian geologists,

> show that the Deccan eruptions began at least 1 million years before K-T time and lasted for at least 1 million years after it, far too long an interval to be consistent with the considerable evidence that the K-T event was rapid. . . . The dinosaurs did not die out well before the K-T boundary [which has been precisely dated], but lived right up to it. . . . Since three Deccan Trap [lava] flows lie below the layer that contains dinosaur remains, the dinosaurs, and presumably the other species that were exterminated in the K-T event, survived at least the first few phases of Deccan volcanism. Thus the eruption of the Deccan volcanoes was not immediately inimical [hostile] to life, even when the volcanoes were right next door.[41]

Another argument against the eruption theory and for the impact one is that the peculiar ratio of the iridium and other rare elements found at the K-T boundary does not match the ratio observed in volcanic material; conversely, it *does* match the ratio seen in extraterrestrial material. "The

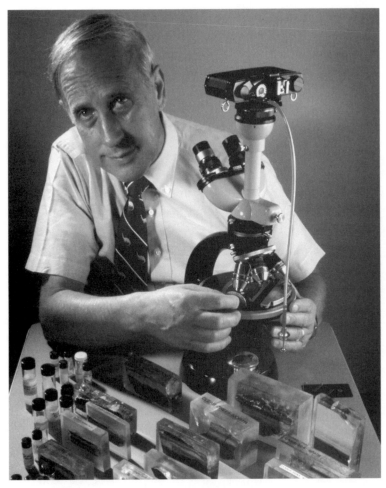

Geologist Glen Izett studies several samples of K-T boundary clays. Scientists have determined that the ratio of gold to iridium in such samples closely matches the gold-iridium ratio in meteorites.

ratio of iridium to elements with similar chemical behavior," say Alvarez and Asaro,

is the same at the boundary layer as it is in meteorites. Miriam Kastner, of the Scripps Institution of Oceanography, [in San Diego, California] working with our group, has determined that the gold-iridium ratio in the carefully studied K-T boundary at Stevns Klint in Denmark agrees to within 5 percent with the ratio in the most primitive meteorites. . . . Indeed, the ratios of all the platinum-group elements found in the K-T boundary give evidence of extraterrestrial origin.[42]

Impact supporters also point to recent studies of large numbers of tiny grains of quartz found at the K-T boundary. Unlike normal quartz samples, these bear "lamellae," bands of deformation caused by the severe shock of extreme pressure and/or moving at tremendous velocities. Scientists usually refer to them as "shocked quartz." Such grains, Alvarez and Asaro argue, are inconsistent with volcanism because they

> are found only in known impact craters, at nuclear test sites, in materials subjected to extreme shock in the laboratory, and in the K-T boundary. . . . Volcanic explosions can produce some deformation [of the quartz grains] but . . . the distinctive multiple lamellae seen in the K-T boundary quartz can only be formed by impact shocks. . . . [Moreover,] eruptions take place at the bottom of the atmosphere; they send material into the high stratosphere at best. . . . Quartz grains, if they came from an eruption, would quickly be slowed by atmospheric drag and fall to the ground. [43]

Still, pro-impact scientists do not discount the part supervolcanism played in the K-T disaster. As Alvarez and Asaro put it,

> The enormous eruptions that created the Deccan Traps did occur during a period spanning the K-T extinction. Further, they represent the greatest outpouring of lava on land in the past quarter of a billion years. . . . No investigator can afford to ignore that kind of coincidence. [44]

Thus, it seems probable that the destructive effects of the impact and eruptions working together made the scope of the catastrophe greater than it would have been had only one of these disasters acted alone. "Dinosaurs were such a large, diverse, and reproductively potent group," says Gregory Paul, that their total extinction at a time when numerous other tetrapods [four-limbed creatures] survived remains amazing. . . . It is possible that it was the combination of events at the time that conspired to do the job. Super-volcanism and increased disease vectors may have reduced the numbers of dinosaurs. Then an impact that would not have killed off an entire healthy dinosaur population caused the population to crash to minimal levels, leaving a battered

Another artist's conception of the K-T impact. A number of scientists contend that this catastrophe along with an event of supervolcanism, brought about the great extinction.

remnant that teetered on the edge of extinction or survival, until chaotic instability wiped out the last breeding individuals. [45]

The Race Is Not to the Swift

Regardless of whether it was the giant impact alone or a combination of the impact and volcanism that exterminated the dinosaurs in the end, what is certain is that the dominant life-form on earth disappeared in what amounts to a geological twinkling of the eye. That left the biological playing field suddenly open to whatever teams of species could best adapt to the new conditions. History has shown that the once small and minimally successful mammals were, overall, the most successful of these teams, for they

The K-T object strikes the earth in the distance as a herd of the horned dinosaur Styracosaurus *react.*

This Apatosaurus *will soon become one of the billions of victims of the K-T impact.*

quite literally inherited the earth in the eons that followed the great disaster.

Furthermore, there is little question that had the K-T catastrophe not occurred, or if it had been less lethal and the dinosaurs had lived, the line of evolution leading to primates and human beings would never have developed. Mammals would likely have remained small, insignificant creatures

Deinosuchus, *the largest known crocodile that ever lived (reaching a length of up to fifty feet) was one of the many non-dinosaurian species wiped out at the end of the Cretaceous period.*

existing as best as they could in the shadow of reptilian giants. "As detectives attempting to unravel this 65-million-year-old mystery," comment Alvarez and Asaro, "we find ourselves pausing from time to time to reflect that we owe our very existence as thinking beings to the impact that destroyed the dinosaurs."[46] Alvarez adds, "Each of us is descended from unknown ancestors who were alive on that day when the fatal rock fell from the sky. They survived and the dinosaurs did not, and that is the reason we are here now—as individuals and as a species."[47]

In contemplating such momentous, far-reaching, and awe-inspiring events, perhaps what stands out most starkly is the deeply ingrained element of randomness and chance involved. If only one or two of the millions of random gravitational and other events that occur daily in the enormous, dark gulfs of cosmic space had happened just a bit differently, the K-T object would have missed the earth, and the dinosaurs would have been spared. (This presumes, of course, that the Deccan eruptions alone were not sufficiently lethal to wipe out the great beasts.)

It was not, therefore, the dinosaurs' own natural shortcomings that struck them down at the height of their power and glory, but an act of blind chance. For paleontologist Kenneth Hsü, this is a potent reminder that advantages such as huge size or superior strength and speed do not always ensure success. Even the most powerful are at the mercy of nature's occasional unexpected, calamitous events, as well as

An illustration of the time before the destructive K-T event, when the dinosaurs reigned the earth.

the ravages of time. "The essence of my perception," Hsü says of the dinosaurs' death in the wake of the K-T event, "can best be expressed by a quote from the Bible: 'I returned and saw under the sun that the race is not to the swift, nor the battle to the strong . . . but time and chance happen to them all.'"[48]

Notes

Introduction: Solving the "Crime" of the Dinosaurs' Death

1. Glenn L. Jepsen, "Riddles of the Terrible Lizards," *American Scientist*, vol. 52, 1964, p. 231.
2. James L. Powell, *Night Comes to the Cretaceous: Comets, Craters, Controversy, and the Last Days of the Dinosaurs*. New York: Harcourt Brace, 1998, pp. xiv–xv.
3. Gregory S. Paul, "The Yucatan Impact and Related Matters," in Gregory S. Paul, ed., *The Scientific American Book of Dinosaurs*. New York: St. Martin's Press, 2000, p. 381.

Chapter One: The First Great Dinosaur Mystery

4. Quoted in John N. Wilford, *The Riddle of the Dinosaur*. New York: Vintage Books, 1985, p. 28.
5. Quoted in Richard Dawkins, *The Blind Watchmaker: Why the Evidence of Evolution Reveals a Universe Without Design*. New York: Norton, 1987, p. 5.
6. Quoted in Wilford, *The Riddle of the Dinosaur*, p. 26.
7. Quoted in Wilford, *The Riddle of the Dinosaur*, p. 37.
8. Quoted in Wilford, *The Riddle of the Dinosaur*, p. 68.

Chapter Two: Initial Explanations for the Dinosaurs' Demise

9. David Norman, *The Illustrated Encyclopedia of Dinosaurs*. New York: Crescent Books, 1985, pp. 194–195.
10. Norman, *The Illustrated Encyclopedia of Dinosaurs*, p. 194.
11. Wilford, *The Riddle of the Dinosaur*, p. 255.
12. Robert T. Bakker, *The Dinosaur Heresies*. New York: William Morrow, 1986, pp. 442–43.
13. Paul, "The Yucatan Impact and Related Matters," pp. 387–88.
14. Kenneth J. Hsü, *The Great Dying*. New York: Ballantine Books, 1986, pp. 106–107.
15. Hsü, *The Great Dying*, p. 103.
16. Norman, *The Illustrated Encyclopedia of Dinosaurs*, p. 197.
17. Paul, "The Yucatan Impact and Related Matters," pp. 389–90.

Chapter Three: Clues to Cosmic Collision

18. Quoted in T. Silver and P. H. Schultz, eds., *Geological Implications of Impacts of Large Asteroids and Comets on the Earth*. Boulder, CO: Geological Society of America, 1982, pp. 415, 421.
19. Powell, *Night Comes to the Cretaceous*, p. 9.
20. Walter Alvarez, *T. Rex and the Crater of Doom*. Princeton, NJ: Princeton University Press, 1997, pp. 40–42.

21. Powell, *Night Comes to the Cretaceous*, pp. 12–13.
22. Alvarez, *T. Rex and the Crater of Doom*, p. 76.
23. Alvarez, *T. Rex and the Crater of Doom*, p. 77.
24. Alvarez, *T. Rex and the Crater of Doom*, p. 75.
25. Powell, *Night Comes to the Cretaceous*, pp. 59–60.
26. Don Lessem, *Kings of Creation: How a New Breed of Scientists Is Revolutionizing Our Understanding of Dinosaurs*. New York: Simon and Schuster, 1992, p. 293.
27. Powell, *Night Comes to the Cretaceous*, p. 121.

Chapter Four: Death from the Sky

28. Powell, *Night Comes to the Cretaceous*, p. 177.
29. Walter Alvarez and Frank Asaro, "An Extraterrestrial Impact," in Paul, *The Scientific American Book of Dinosaurs*, p. 351.
30. Powell, *Night Comes to the Cretaceous*, p. 177.
31. Alvarez and Asaro, "An Extraterrestrial Impact," p. 351.
32. Powell, *Night Comes to the Cretaceous*, p. 178.
33. Alvarez and Asaro, "An Extraterrestrial Impact," p. 352.
34. David M. Raup, *Extinction: Bad Genes or Bad Luck?* New York: Norton, 1991, p. 191.

Chapter Five: The Debate Continues

35. Luis W. Alvarez, "Experimental Evidence That an Asteroid Impact Led to the Extinction of Many Species 65 Million Years Ago," *Proceedings of the National Academy of Sciences*, vol. 80, 1983, p. 639.
36. Vincent E. Courtillot, "A Volcanic Eruption," in Paul, *The Scientific American Book of Dinosaurs*, p. 359.
37. Courtillot, "A Volcanic Eruption," p. 364.
38. Courtillot, "A Volcanic Eruption," p. 360.
39. Wilford, *The Riddle of the Dinosaur*, pp. 253–54.
40. Alvarez, *T. Rex and the Crater of Doom*, p. 143.
41. Powell, *Night Comes to the Cretaceous*, pp. 92–93.
42. Alvarez and Asaro, "An Extraterrestrial Impact," pp. 349–50.
43. Alvarez and Asaro, "An Extraterrestrial Impact," pp. 350, 355.
44. Alvarez and Asaro, "An Extraterrestrial Impact," pp. 355–56.
45. Paul, "The Yucatan Impact and Related Matters," p. 390.
46. Alvarez and Asaro, "An Extraterrestrial Impact," p. 357.
47. Alvarez, *T. Rex and the Crater of Doom*, p. 130.
48. Hsü, *The Great Dying*, p. 281.

For Further Reading

Roy Chapman Andrews, *All About Dinosaurs.* New York: Random House, 1953. Although this older book is now woefully out-of-date in many respects, it was in its time a fascinating view of dinosaurs written for young readers by one of the last great adventurer-fossil hunters, whose expeditions became legendary. More important, the book retains some historical significance as one of the main works that first introduced many of today's scientists and science writers to dinosaurs. It is still available in a few larger libraries, so those libraries that do not have it can order it through interlibrary loan.

Isaac Asimov, *Death from Space: What Killed the Dinosaurs?* Milwaukee, WI: Gareth Stevens, 1994. The late Dr. Asimov, one of the twentieth century's leading explainers of science for general readers, delivers an intriguing and entertaining exploration of the causes of the mass extinction that did in the dinosaurs.

Peter Dodson, *An Alphabet of Dinosaurs.* New York: Scholastic, 1995. Introduces twenty-six dinosaurs to young readers, with a brief but informative text and excellent color paintings for each dinosaur.

J. Lynett Gillette, *Dinosaur Ghosts: The Mystery of Coelophysis.* New York: Dial Books for Young Readers, 1997. Describes the dinosaur called Coelophysis and how the remains of a number of its kind were discovered in New Mexico in the twentieth century. A good deal of space is devoted to speculation about how these animals died.

Douglas Henderson, *Asteroid Impact.* New York: Dial Books for Young Readers, 2000. An excellent, beautifully illustrated synopsis of the asteroid impact theory of the extinction of the dinosaurs aimed at basic and intermediate young readers. Highly recommended.

Patricia Lauber, *How Dinosaurs Came to Be.* New York: Simon and Schuster, 1996. Explores the early evolution of life on earth, including the rise of the dinosaurs.

William Lindsay, ed., *American Museum of Natural History: On the Trail of Incredible Dinosaurs.* New York: Dorling Kindersley, 1998. Describes a few dinosaurs in some detail, explains how paleontologists pieced together their skeletons and other evidence, and briefly speculates about how these creatures died.

Peter Zallinger, *Dinosaurs and Other Archosaurs.* New York: Random House, 1999. An updated edition of Zallinger's fine 1986 book surveying the major kinds of dinosaurs.

Howard Zimmerman and George Olshevsky, *Dinosaurs: The Biggest, Baddest, Strongest, Fastest*. Springfield, IL: Atheneum, 2000. A striking oversized picture book with more than seventy-five stunning, accurate illustrations of some of the more fascinating dinosaur species. The text is up-to-date, with information on the latest scientific theories about these ancient beasts. Highly recommended.

Major Works Consulted

Luis W. Alvarez, Walter Alvarez, et al., "Extraterrestrial Cause for the Cretaceous-Tertiary Extinction," *Science*, vol. 208, 1980. A major early article outlining the impact scenario by the scientists who originated this controversial theory for the demise of the dinosaurs.

Walter Alvarez, *T. Rex and the Crater of Doom*. Princeton, NJ: Princeton University Press, 1997. A thorough and riveting summary of the impact theory's major tenets written by one of its originators. Highly recommended.

Michael J. Benton, "Scientific Methodologies in Collision: The History of the Study of the Extinction of the Dinosaurs," *Evolutionary Biology*, vol. 24, 1990. Offers an informative synopsis of how the major theories about dinosaur extinction developed.

David B. Carlisle, *Dinosaurs, Diamonds, and Things from Outer Space*. Stanford, CA: Stanford University Press, 1995. Canadian scientist David Carlisle presents geochemical evidence supporting the impact theory for the K-T event and suggests why some species became extinct while others survived.

William Glenn, ed., *The Mass Extinction Debates: How Science Works in a Crisis*. Stanford, CA: Stanford University Press, 1994. A riveting overview of the often bitter debate between those scientists supporting the impact theory and those against it (from the late 1970s to the early 1990s). Highly recommended.

Donald Goldsmith, *Nemesis: The Death Star and Other Theories of Mass Extinction*. New York: Berkeley Books, 1985. This is a well-written look at the controversial and still unproven thesis that a dim companion of the sun lurks on the edge of the solar system and periodically nudges comets into earth-crossing orbits. Includes a good deal of information about cometary bombardment of earth and how it may have affected life on the planet.

Kenneth J. Hsü, *The Great Dying*. New York: Ballantine Books, 1986. Discusses the phenomenon of extinction and various theories attempting to explain the causes of prehistoric mass extinctions, including the cometary impact theory.

Richard A. Kerr, "A Bigger Death Knell for the Dinosaurs?" *Science*, September 17, 1993. Explores the possibility that the K-T event might have been larger in scope than originally postulated by scientists.

David H. Levy, Eugene M. Shoemaker, et al., "Comet Shoemaker-Levy 9 Meets

Jupiter," *Scientific American*, vol. 273, 1995. Summarizes initial findings about the magnitude of the impacts made on the planet Jupiter by the fragments of a comet, giving scientists a firsthand look at the same kind of catastrophe that probably killed the dinosaurs.

Digby McClean, "Asteroid or Volcano: Have the Volcanists Been Heard?" *Science*, vol. 259, 1993. Makes the case that much of the evidence suggesting that the K-T event was caused by an extraterrestrial impact might be explained instead by an episode of supervolcanism.

Virginia Morell, "How Lethal Was the K-T Impact?" *Science*, September 17, 1993. Attempts to estimate the overall size and killing power of the K-T event based on available evidence.

Charles B. Officer and Jake Page, *The Great Dinosaur Extinction Controversy*. Reading, MA: Addison-Wesley, 1996. Officer, the major remaining opponent of the extraterrestrial impact theory, offers arguments against that theory and concludes that major volcanic events are a more likely culprit in the dinosaurs' demise.

Gregory S. Paul, ed., *The Scientific American Book of Dinosaurs*. New York: St. Martin's Press, 2000. An excellent overview of present knowledge about dinosaurs, including several essays by noted scientists about the two major competing extinction theories—extraterrestrial impact and supervolcanism.

James L. Powell, *Night Comes to the Cretaceous: Comets, Craters, Controversy, and the Last Days of the Dinosaurs*. New York: Harcourt Brace, 1998. The most comprehensive available general summary of the debate about dinosaur extinction. Powell presents the evidence gathered so far for the impact theory and gives plenty of space to its few detractors. Highly recommended.

David M. Raup, *Extinction: Bad Genes or Bad Luck?* New York: Norton, 1991. Raup, a distinguished University of Chicago scholar, delivers a fascinating, very informative discussion of the process of extinction. Is it more often caused by inherent genetic defects or is it just a matter of chance and unfortunate timing? Or is it some combination of these factors? An important book.

Gerrit L. Verschuur, *Impact: The Threat of Comets and Asteroids*. New York: Oxford University Press, 1996. A well-researched and well-written examination of the real threat of extraterrestrial bombardment of the earth, which many scientists now believe may be a recurring cause of mass extinctions.

John N. Wilford, *The Riddle of the Dinosaur*. New York: Vintage Books, 1985. A superior general overview of dinosaurs, with much excellent historical material on the discovery of the beasts and the early fossil hunters.

Additional Works Consulted

Luis W. Alvarez, *Adventures of a Physicist.* New York: Basic Books, 1987.

———, "Experimental Evidence That an Asteroid Impact Led to the Extinction of Many Species 65 Million Years Ago," *Proceedings of the National Academy of Sciences,* vol. 80, 1983.

Walter Alvarez and Frank Asaro, "An Extraterrestrial Impact," *Scientific American,* vol. 263, 1990.

J. D. Archibald, *Dinosaur Extinction and the End of an Era: What the Fossils Say.* New York: Columbia University Press, 1996.

Isaac Azimov, *A Choice of Catastrophes.* New York: Simon and Schuster, 1979.

———, *Counting the Eons.* New York: Avon Books, 1983.

———, *Did Comets Kill the Dinosaurs?* Milwaukee, WI: Gareth Stevens, 1988.

Robert T. Bakker, *The Dinosaur Heresies.* New York: William Morrow, 1986.

Michael J. Benton, "Late Triassic Extinctions and the Origin of the Dinosaurs," *Science,* May 7, 1993.

Richard Dawkins, *The Blind Watchmaker: Why the Evidence of Evolution Reveals a Universe Without Design.* New York: Norton, 1987.

Dougal Dixon et al., *The Macmillan Illustrated Encyclopedia of Dinosaurs and Prehistoric Animals.* New York: Macmillan, 1988.

S. Gartner and J. P. McGuirk, "Terminal Cretaceous Extinction Scenario for a Catastrophe," *Science,* vol. 206, 1979.

William Glen, "What Killed the Dinosaurs?" *American Scientists,* July/August 1990.

Stephen Jay Gould, *Bully for Brontosaurus: Reflections on Natural History.* New York: Norton, 1991.

L. J. Hickey, "Land Plant Evidence Compatible with Gradual, Not Catastrophic, Change at the End of the Cretaceous," *Nature,* vol. 292, 1981.

John R. Horner, *Digging Dinosaurs.* New York: Workman, 1988.

Glenn L. Jepsen, "Riddles of the Terrible Lizards," *American Scientist,* vol. 52, 1964.

Richard A. Kerr, "Extraterrestrial Impact Gets More Support," *Science,* vol. 236, 1987.

Don Lessem, *Kings of Creation: How a New Breed of Scientists Is Revolutionizing Our Understanding of Dinosaurs.* New York: Simon and Schuster, 1992.

John S. Lewis, *Rain of Iron and Ice: The Very Real Threat of Comet and Asteroid*

Bombardment. Reading, MA: Addison-Wesley, 1996.

David Norman, *The Illustrated Encyclopedia of Dinosaurs.* New York: Crescent Books, 1985.

Charles B. Officer and N. L. Carter, "A Review of the Structure, Petrology, and Dynamic Deformation Characteristics of Some Enigmatic Terrestrial Structures," *Earth-Science Reviews,* vol. 30, 1991.

Charles B. Officer and Charles L. Drake, "The Cretaceous-Tertiary Transition," *Science,* vol. 219, 1983.

———, "Terminal Cretaceous Environmental Events," *Science,* vol. 227, 1985.

K. O. Pope, A. C. Ocampo, et al., "Mexican Site for K/T Impact Crater," *Nature,* vol. 351, 1991.

Byron Preiss and Robert Silverberg, eds., *The Ultimate Dinosaur.* New York: Bantam Books, 1992.

David M. Raup, *Nemesis Affair: A Story of the Death of Dinosaurs and the Ways of Science.* New York: Norton, 1986.

David M. Raup and J. J. Sepkoski Jr., "Periodicity of Extinctions in the Geologic Past," *Proceedings of the National Academy of Sciences of the United States of America,* vol. 81, 1984.

D. A. Russell, "The Enigma of the Extinction of the Dinosaurs," *Annual Review of Earth and Planetary Sciences,* vol. 7, 1979.

T. Silver and P. H. Schultz, eds., *Geological Implications of Impacts of Large Asteroids and Comets on the Earth.* Boulder, CO: Geological Society of America, 1982.

Harold C. Urey, "Cometary Collisions and Geological Periods," *Nature,* vol. 242, 1973.

———, "For Dinosaur Extinction Theory, a 'Smoking Gun,'" *New York Times,* February 7, 1991.

Index

Picture Credits

Cover photo: Photo Researchers, Inc./SPL/Chris Butler
American Museum of Natural History, 33, 94
American Museum of Natural History/R. E. Logan, 11
American Museum of Natural History/E. M. Fulda, 37
Archive Photos, 86
Corbis, 82
Corbis/AFP, 44
Corbis/Tom Bean, 19
Corbis/Bettmann, 21, 25, 27
Corbis/Jonathan Blair, 89
Corbis/Premium Stock, 91
Corbis/Roger Ressmeyer, 49
Corbis/Reuters NewMedia, Inc., 61
NASA, 64
Photo Researchers, Inc., 54
Photo Researchers, Inc./John Foster, 81
Photo Researchers, Inc./Francois Gohier, 31, 51
Photo Researchers, Inc./George Kagawa, 52
Photo Researchers, Inc./Steve A. Munsinger, 92
Photo Researchers, Inc./Richard T. Nowitz, 23
Photo Researchers, Inc./Stephen and Donna O'Meara, 56
Photo Researchers, Inc./Soames Summerhays, 85
Science Photo Library, 22
Science Photo Library/Julian Baum, 62, 93
Science Photo Library/Chris Butler, 69, 79, 95
Science Photo Library/David A. Hardy, 66
Science Photo Library/Ludek Pesek, 39, 40
Science Photo Library/D. Van Ravenswaay, 15, 55, 71, 73, 77
Science Photo Library/Joe Tucciarone, 34, 68, 72
Science Photo Library/Victor Habbick Visions, 75
U.S. Geological Survey, 13

About the Author

In addition to his acclaimed volumes on ancient civilizations, historian Don Nardo has published several studies examining the modern discovery of biological evolution and extinction, among them *The Origin of Species: Darwin's Theory of Evolution, Dinosaurs: Unearthing the Secrets of Ancient Beasts*, and a biography of Darwin, as well as an overview of the famous Scopes trial, which focused on the legitimacy of teaching evolution in schools. Mr. Nardo lives with his wife, Christine, in Massachusetts.